DAVID NETH

FUSE

OMERTÀ

BOOK 2

Omertà
Fuse, Book 2
Copyright © 2018 by David Neth
Batavia, NY

www.DavidNethBooks.com

Publisher: David Neth
Editing: Amy Maddox of The Blue Pencil
Proofreading: John Ognibene

ISBN: 978-1-945336-88-1
First edition

Subscribe to the author's newsletter for updates and exclusive content:
DavidNethBooks.com/Newsletter

Follow the author at:
www.facebook.com/DavidNethBooks
www.twitter.com/DavidNethBooks
www.instagram.com/dneth13

Also by David Neth

<u>Fuse Series</u>
Origin

<u>Small Town Christmas Series</u>
A Christmas Reunion

<u>Under the Moon Series</u>
The Full Moon

The Harvest Moon

The Blood Moon

The Crescent Moon

The Blue Moon

The Art of Magic

<u>Anthology</u>
Collateral Damage:
A Superhero Anthology

<u>Short Stories</u>
Limelight

Snow After Christmas

<u>Nonfiction</u>
Go Indie: A Guide to Your First
Year Self-Publishing

Chapter One

I don't move while Dean kisses me. No reaction. Nothing.

It's a surprise, that's for sure. One minute I'm grieving the loss of my girlfriend, who, as of this morning, was still lying in the First Olympian Medical Center recovering from her attack a few weeks ago. Now I'm sitting on the floor of my apartment, tears in my eyes, kissing a man I only met a few weeks ago. A man I know is dangerous.

A *man*.

Finally I pull away.

"Um…" I stutter. "What was that?" The loss of Emma has drained me for the moment. I pull away from him, desperate to put space between us.

"Sorry." He leans back against the wall, running his hands through his short dark hair.

I should say something more. Did he mean to kiss me? It was a long kiss, of course he did. Does he have feelings for me or did he just get caught up in the moment? Maybe he was just trying to distract me for a minute. Trying to console me. Trying to get my mind off everything that happened tonight.

Fuse: Omertà

How I found out Dean's father is none other than Carlo Martelli, the man in charge of the powerful crime family in Olympia. The family connected to Michael Bello, who sent two men after Emma to rape her.

But still, Dean's reaction doesn't make sense. Emma's the one I'm grieving. My *girlfriend*. I don't have an interest in Dean. Or any man, for that matter. I'm not—

Keys fumble in the hallway and we both scramble to our feet.

"Ethan," Cale says as he and his girlfriend, Myra, come through the door.

My brother takes my face in his hands and studies me. My swollen, black-and-blue eye, cut cheek, and bloodshot eyes. All a result of my alter ego, Fuse, helping put away Bello.

"What the hell happened?" he asks. "Did you get jumped again?"

"Nothing. It's fine." I try to pull away from him, but he wraps me in a hug, and finally I lean into it.

Myra rubs my back. "We just heard. Oh, Ethan, I'm so sorry."

Another wave of sadness hits me as Cale moves away for Myra to hug me.

"How are you holding up?" he asks.

Words fail me, and all I can do is shake my head. His eyes linger on my face, but he doesn't say anything.

"Are you hungry?" Cale asks. "I can order something."

"No," I mutter.

I wipe at my face in an attempt to hide my misery. I hate being the center of attention like this. For this reason. They're just trying to comfort me, but I just need space.

Well, Cale and Myra are just trying to comfort me. I don't know what Dean was thinking, blindsiding me like that. I still can't meet his eyes.

Still, their efforts can only go so far. At the end of the day, all I want is Emma.

"Let's just sit down." Myra leads us to the couch, and she and Cale sit on either side of me.

Dean nervously sits in the chair to our right. I don't quite know what to make of him. As much help as he's been these last few weeks, I'm glad he's here. But after what Alex and Tucker told me earlier, not to mention that kiss, I'm all sorts of confused right now.

After a few minutes of silence, Cale turns on the TV. I guess they don't know what to say, so their company is all I get. I'm glad. The TV takes everyone's attention off of me.

Cale channel surfs until we settle on one of the Harry Potter movies. Nobody seems to be paying attention, though. Cale and Myra keep stealing glances at me and exchanging looks with one another. I pretend not to notice, though my eyes keep drifting to Dean.

That kiss was surprising, inappropriate, and uncalled for. He might not have ever met Emma, but he knew about her. He should've known he was crossing a line.

"Come on, let's go," Myra says, breaking into my thoughts. She snatches the remote from Cale and clicks off the TV. "We all have to work tomor—" She stops. My brother must've told her that I'm recently unemployed. Another blow to my life.

Cale stretches and yawns. "If you want us to do something together tomorrow, Ethan, I can work from home for a bit. I might have to move some appointments around, but we can make it work."

I shake my head. "No thanks. I'll be fine."

I don't know what I'm going to do, but I know I want to be alone. At least for a little bit.

"You sure?" Myra asks. "It's okay if you need someone. This isn't the time to be brave. You're going to feel different when you wake up to an empty apartment."

"Thanks, but—"

"I don't have any patients tomorrow," Dean adds. "I can stay home if you want."

"Guys, I don't need to be babysat," I finally say. "Just…give me some time."

I head off to the bathroom to start getting ready for bed. When I'm done, Cale and Myra take my place at the sink to brush their teeth. Meanwhile, Dean hangs out awkwardly by the door.

"Do you want me to go, or…" he whispers to me.

I let out a breath of air and study him. Too many emotions flow through me. I can't keep track of them all. I'm not exactly happy with Dean, but he's the only one who fully understands everything on my plate right now. And I can't add even more guilt to my conscience by kicking him out on the street in the middle of the night. He may have crossed the line with that kiss, but he did just save my life.

"No, you can stay," I tell him.

He nods. "Thanks. And again, I'm sorry. About Emma. About what happened earlier." He stares at the floor.

"Yeah, well…" I don't know what to say.

Myra emerges from the bathroom and takes my hand. "Ethan, if you need anything—"

"I'll be fine. Thank you, though."

Cale returns and gives me another hug. "It'll be okay, little brother," he mutters against my ear. I squeeze him tighter for a minute and then let go.

"Still okay with the couch?" he asks Dean.

"Yeah. Thanks again for letting me stay."

Cale looks at me briefly before turning back to Dean. "No problem."

With another pat on the shoulder, Cale leads Myra back to their room for the night and I head back to mine.

Dean starts making up his bed on the couch.

I linger, wanting to say something to assure him we're okay. Well, maybe not okay, but I'm not mad at him. Not really. I don't know how I feel. All I know is I'm glad he's here.

"Hey, are you all right?" Dean asks.

I wipe at my eyes, embarrassed. I didn't even realize I was crying.

"I know it's harder at night, but just try to think of anything else," he adds. "You need sleep. It's only going to help."

I nod, but still the tears flow. I can't help it. I'm lost and I don't know how I can fix it.

"Hey, come here."

I let him pull me into a hug. After a moment, I lift my arms and return it, even squeezing him tighter the longer it lasts. I've never been a hugger, but this, and the ones I got from my brother and Myra, are nice. Comforting.

He pulls away. "I know you're probably upset with me right now, but if there's anything you need—*anything*—I'm here. I mean it. I know what it's like to lose someone close like that."

"Thanks, Dean." I sniffle and wipe my nose in the back of my hand. "I should get some sleep."

"Yeah. Good night."

I close my bedroom door and get under the covers.

Emma's gone.

The reality hits me with unexpected ferocity, and I sob silently into my pillow, shoulders shaking. I don't want anyone to hear.

I've already lived three weeks without her, since she was unconscious in the hospital, but now it's official. I'm never going to see her, never going to hold her or talk to her. She wasn't just my girlfriend, she was my best friend. And now she's gone.

After a while the tears ease off. I take a shuddering breath, wipe my face with the sheet, and roll onto my back. And instead of Emma's face, I see Michael Bello's, the pig who arranged her attack. He was arrested for what he did, but is that enough? He's probably been arrested before. Why would this time be any different? And does a lifetime in prison—*if* that's what he gets—compare to the life sentence Emma got? Even if I wipe out Bello's operations in the Martelli family empire, it'll never bring Emma back.

And then there's Dean. I kick off the covers, tuck my arm under my pillow, and roll back onto my side. The last twelve hours have been up and down with him. He was my friend and ally this morning, then Alex and Tucker told me he's the son of Carlo Martelli, and then he saved me from Bello's men and kissed me.

I can't believe he kissed me.

I stare at the city lights reflecting on the ceiling. Emma's bedroom didn't have this much light shining in it. Or noise. My apartment is right next to I-23, or the Wind Tunnel, as we Olympians know it. At night there's a lot of light and ambient noise.

Fuse: Omertà

Emma never liked staying here because of the noise. And because of Cale. Even I preferred to stay at her place because it was nicer and quieter, and it was just the two of us.

That's never going to happen again. Emma's sister, Theresa, might call me to help clean out her apartment or something else to help settle her affairs. But after that and the funeral, all I'll have are memories. I'll never hear the sound of her laugh. Feel her soft hands. Wake up next to her.

The bed suddenly feels huge without Emma. I cling to the pillow for closeness and let myself be consumed in her memory. At least for a little while, I'm allowed.

But I know that what happened to Emma was not a unique event. There'll be other attacks like hers. I can only hope to put an end to some of them. In that sense, I'll be keeping her memory alive by fighting for her.

———

THIS DRUG DEALER is faster than I thought. It's a good thing I'm not as pudgy as I was a couple months ago, I think as I race down Lincoln Avenue in Hopman.

He rounds a corner and I follow, noticing that this is the first time it's snowed all year. To be honest, I don't mind the cold. Not right now, at least. I thought it'd work against me with my dark Fuse suit, but as I move between the shadows, my footsteps are softer and quieter than those of the dealer.

After the relentless sympathetic texts and phone calls all day, I needed to get out of the house and do something as Fuse. I snuck out just before everyone came home from work and could dole out the sympathies in person. Luckily—if you could call it that—I stumbled on some suspicious activity almost as soon as I got into the Hopman neighborhood. In the span of ten minutes I watched the street, I saw three cars pull up to one house, run inside for a minute before pulling away again.

Idiots. At least they were smart about one thing: the deal was made inside out of sight. Not that it wasn't obvious to figure out what they were doing.

Chapter One

Just as I was about to break into the dealer's house and bust him, he walked out to have a cigarette.

"Is that as bad as it gets for you or do you dip into your inventory as well?" I said when I snuck up on him.

He took off running from there and I still haven't caught up to him.

I wait until he turns down a narrow side street to send a streak of lightning at his feet. Not to hit him, just to scare him.

He pauses long enough for me to collide into him and pin him on the cold ground.

I know I shouldn't go looking for trouble—my battered face is a reminder of that—but I need to do something. Bello had control over the gangs in Hopman. At least, he had influence over them. Just because he's been arrested doesn't mean they have disbanded. Hopman is still a dangerous place, and this dealer is proof of that.

"What's your name?" I ask as I search him for a weapon. I feel something long and flat in his pocket and pull out a short knife.

"Fuck off."

I shove his face against the cracked sidewalk. It's cold enough that the snow is just starting to stick. Good.

Pressing the com in my ear, I call the police.

"This is Fuse," I murmur in my disguised voice. "I have a drug dealer on Donald Avenue, chased him from his house on Lincoln. I'll leave him waiting for you."

"What? No, man, this ain't right! You can't just leave me here! I didn't do nothing!"

I reach around and unbuckle his belt.

"What the fuck, man!"

Once his belt is free, I use it to tie up his hands. I really need to start carrying handcuffs or some rope with me.

"Didn't do anything, huh? Then why did you take off running when you saw me?" I ask him.

He's quiet again.

"Who else is working with you?"

Still nothing. He struggles under my weight, swinging his

feet, trying to free himself. I push down harder.

I wish I knew who this guy was or who else he could be working with. Or for. That way I could go after his friends tonight before they got word that I've intervened.

When I see the police cars coming from the end of the street, I mutter to the dealer, "Good luck," before taking off.

The clinic's not far from here, and my chest burns from breathing in the cold air, so I walk the few blocks, letting my heart rate return to normal. I punch in the security code and let myself in.

It's late. Just after midnight. I should probably go back out and look for more gang members to bring them in, but I can't help but feel like I'd be running in blind. And how do I know I'm bringing in the right guys?

Throughout the day I've been outlining an idea for facial recognition software. Something that would help me speed up my search for criminals within the Grid. I think I've managed to figure out how to search the police database, city records, hospital records, everything. Sometimes even the most minor detail can help connect the dots in a case.

Flicking on the basement light, I pull off my mask as I head down the stairs. I hit the power button on the computer and, while I'm waiting for it to boot up, jot down my ideas. If I can pull someone's image off a street camera and use that to search through several databases, I'd be able to at least identify who I'm going after.

Once the computer kicks up, I begin putting together the software. Luckily, I'm able to use some of the source code from similar programs and simply modify it, but it's still a long process. Really long, actually. It's not until my eyes burn and my back aches that I realize I've been working all night. It's almost five in the morning by time I turn off the lights, reset the alarm, and head for home.

———

Chapter One

THE COLD NOVEMBER rain is very fitting today. Emma's funeral. Even though each of the pallbearers have umbrellas, we still get wet. Which is why I immediately take off my suit jacket when we get to the reception hall after the service. We're out in Terry Lake, where Emma's parents live. They wanted her to be buried close to them.

It's been three days since she died. The calling hours were yesterday and even though I didn't know very many of the people who came—family, mostly—it was the hardest two hours of my life. Standing in the line with Emma's family, like we were on public display. Smiling and trying to downplay how upset I was. I would've taken more of a beating from Bello and his men in exchange for Emma's calling hours.

My face is actually a big topic of conversation today. Since nobody really knows me, it serves as a good icebreaker.

"I don't normally look like this," I tell them. "I just got in a car accident."

The car accident excuse works with everyone except Cale and Myra.

"How did you *really* get hurt?" my brother asks when I join them at our table. "It was a thug, wasn't it?"

"Cale, not now," Myra berates, although she continues to study my injuries.

Theresa comes over, saving me from further explanation.

"Thanks for coming, you guys," she says to my brother and Myra. "Emma said she did a lot with Ethan and his family. It's really nice that you could be here."

"Of course," Myra says against Theresa's ear as she hugs her. "I know it's been a rough week."

That it has. Since she passed I feel like I've been stuck in a pit of grief. I don't have any better handle on my life. I've kept myself buried in the basement of the clinic, working on the software. Alex has been giving me a pass because of Emma, no longer pursuing my "eviction" in the wake of my grief. Which meant that I was mostly left alone to set up a police scanner. I also tapped into their network and arrest files to help me find possible repeat offenders.

Theresa hugs me for what seems like the millionth time today. "How are you holding up?"

I bury my hands in my pockets and shrug. "You know."

She gives me a sympathetic nod. "Yeah. Give me a call sometime if you want to talk, okay?"

"Okay."

She cups my face in one of her hands. "Did you get this looked at?"

I pull away. "Yeah," I lie. "Just have to keep icing it."

Theresa gives me a sad smile and looks back to Cale and Myra. "Thanks again for coming."

The attention my face draw only serves as a reminder of the way Bello and his men so easily overpowered me. I need to work on my skill as a crimefighter. I've been practicing, and I managed to catch a couple petty criminals using the new system. The suit Wes made me helps regulate my powers more so I can zap people without severely hurting them. Last night I even figured out how to get my powers to stun one guy, like he'd been tased.

"So, Dean says you haven't been around much since…you know," Cale says after Myra leaves to get us some drinks.

I narrow my eyes. "Since when are you and Dean best friends?"

"Come on, Ethan, we just want to make sure you're doing okay."

"I'm fine."

"Are you ever going to tell me how you really got hurt?" He indicates my battered face, which is doing much better. The swelling has gone down and the bruise is starting to fade.

"Cale, just don't worry about it. I'm fine."

"Okay." He leans back and crosses his arms. "So you can start looking for a job then, right?"

"I don't know. I guess."

"I'm going to need more than that, Ethan. I'm trying to help." When I don't respond, he continues, "Myra and I have been talking, and we think you getting out of the house is a good thing, but we're worried about what you're doing."

"Nothing illegal." Well, not really.

Chapter One

"That's not what I was thinking, but thanks for putting *that* thought into my head. But wandering around by yourself when you're this upset…" He shrugs. "I don't know, just seems stupid. I've never really lost anyone close to me before, but I can imagine that nothing seems worth it right now. Getting a job will help."

Really? Here? I look around the room at the other mourners in black, some still crying from the funeral, others giving endless hugs to one another. This is when he decides to give me the "get a job" lecture? I've only been unemployed for a week. Not to mention my girlfriend just died. Can't he cut me some slack?

"You just want me to pay the rent," I say.

"Well, yeah. I'm barely making it on my own since your paychecks have been hit or miss lately. I don't *need* that apartment. I could move in with Myra. *You'd* be the one without a place to live."

I ball my fists. I want to shout at him, but Myra stops me.

"What's going on?" she whisper-yells.

"I was telling Ethan how it'd be beneficial for him to get a job," Cale explains.

Myra sets down the drinks. "Ethan," she says, placing a hand on my shoulder, "it's not that we're trying to rush you into anything you're not ready for, it's just that we thought it'd give you a sense of purpose. And finding a job—especially after you were let go—can take awhile. Best to get started early."

Tapping the table with my finger, I stare at them until there's silence. "Are you done?"

Myra looks at me with sad eyes, which drives me crazy. She thinks I'm so fragile. I don't need to be handled with kid gloves. I just need space.

"I'll look into that job lead with Tranidek. Until then, I'd appreciate it if you leave me the fuck alone." With that, I stand and walk out to get some air.

Chapter Two

The Rivalry is the last place I want to be tonight, with the rowdy college crowd and loud music. Well, maybe not the very last. Definitely bottom ten I think to myself as I un-stick my shoes from the floor. Apparently my misery has given Dean and Cale something to talk about. They've concocted this plan to go out to the bar to help me get my mind off Emma.

I appreciate their efforts, but things between me and Dean are still weird, and I can't talk to Cale about most of the things that go on in my life. He doesn't know what I've been through in the last month and a half as Fuse. If I were to tell him, I know I'd get a lecture and I'd worry him. Not to mention, there's no way in hell I'd tell him about the kiss. The teasing, the insinuations, the suspicion that would result. Nope, not having it.

"So how did you get into physical therapy?" Cale asks Dean after a long period of no conversation. We each have a bottle in front of us, but I don't feel like drinking. My hands are wet from the condensation dripping down the bottle.

"I played football in high school for a bit," he responds. "Treating sports injuries was what I knew when I first went to college. Not to mention it's more stable than a football scholarship. I guess I just became more interested in it the more I learned."

"And you must be good at it, too," Cale says with a laugh. "You turned my brother into a gym rat." He smacks my arm, but I don't smile. "Come on, Ethan. I'm just teasing. You're looking good since you started working out. Keep it up."

"Thanks." I glance at Dean before taking a sip of my drink.

Dean and I haven't worked out together—or really done anything together—since Tuesday when Emma died. I've mostly been running every morning for exercise. Around Chester Park, chasing petty criminals, whenever I need to kill time at night to make sure Dean's asleep. The little definition in my muscles I was developing before is gone now. But at least my stamina is still up.

"What about you?" Dean asks. "How'd you get into reporting?"

Cale shrugs. "Took a newspaper class as an elective in college. Discovered I hate writing but love news. So I switched to TV."

"That's cool," Dean says with a nod.

"Yeah."

The three of us are quiet again. It's because of me this outing is awkward. I'm being a wet blanket. I'm pouting because I don't want to be here, and it's not fair to them.

"Any new leads on the Works story?" I ask my brother, swallowing my pride—and a swig of my beer.

"Actually, yeah." He lights up a little, which makes me smile. "I have a meeting with the developer of the housing project."

"It's not someone from Michael Bello's camp, is it?" Dean asks.

"No, but he's been a hot topic at the station. Everyone wants to be on that story, or at least get approval to sit in on the trial." He takes a sip before continuing. "No, the guy I'm meeting is Leon Wallace. He's done some other projects throughout the city."

"Leon Wallace?" I shoot a look to Dean. He looks just as scared as I am.

Cale looks between us. "Do you guys know him?"

I straighten up and sip my drink.

"No," Dean responds. "Not really, anyway. He's just been in the paper a lot for his different projects."

Cale studies us. "What's going on with you two?"

"Nothing," I say a little too fast.

He smirks. "Trouble in paradise, lovebirds?"

My stomach hollows out and my whole body flashes with heat. Does he know about the kiss? No, how would he? Did Dean tell him?

"Guys, I'm kidding," Cale adds with a laugh. "Geez, with the looks on your faces you'd think there *was* something going on."

"Sorry I'm late," Myra says as she joins us at our small table, saving me from coming up with a response. She pulls off her coat and smiles brightly. "I have some awesome news!"

Cale turns his attention to her, his eyes lighting up as well. "You got it?"

She nods and wraps her arms around his neck, squeezing tight.

"What's going on?" I wipe my wet hands onto my jeans.

Myra lets go of my brother and turns back to the table. "Okay, so I'm sure you know how my boss got arrested for conspiring with the Martelli family and killing proposals related to the Hopman District."

"Based off evidence *you* put together," I add. "Yeah, I'm aware."

"Well, that left an open spot on city council. I just got an email and…" She pauses, smiling at the three of us waiting in suspense. "…last night the rest of the councilmembers voted for me to fill in as interim councilmember!"

"Myra, that's great!" I pull her into a hug. "You deserve this."

"Yeah, but it's going to be a ton of work if I want this to be permanent. There's going to be a special election next month for the official councilmember."

"That's right before the holidays," Dean adds.

"I know," she says with a cringe. "But they want the new person in before the new year, and I guess there are a couple potential candidates they're thinking of already." She shrugs. "Ultimately, it comes down to the vote."

"But if they made you interim councilwoman, they must be favoring you, right?" Cale asks.

"I hope so, but they might've just given it to me because I was Frank Lloyd's assistant. Basically, I think they just want me to hold down the fort until the election."

"But you'd be perfect for this job!" Cale gushes.

"Thanks, sweetie, but this is going to be a really hectic month."

"Have you already thought of things to tip the odds in your favor?" I tap the bottle cap against the tabletop.

"Of course. I've had this laundry list of ideas since I started working for Frank Lloyd. The problem is, his shady tactics have burned some bridges. I'm not sure I'll be able to get the funding or community support for some of the initiatives I have in mind. At least, not quick enough for the council to take notice. But I hope I can change some people's minds."

Cale wraps his arm around her and gives a quick squeeze. "I'm sure you'll think of something. It's about time someone honest got into city hall."

"Monday, the work begins," she says.

"But tonight, we celebrate. I'm going to get the next round." With a tap of the table, Cale turns and heads back toward the bar.

For the first time since Emma passed, a genuine smile spreads across my face. All I can do is look for the positive outcomes of the night Emma died. Myra becoming a councilwoman—even if it's temporary—is a very good thing.

———

THE COLD RAIN pelting my face keeps me alert as I jog to the clinic the next morning. We didn't get back from the bar until after one in the morning. Myra slept over since our apartment is only a few blocks away from the bar, so Cale was distracted. And Dean and I were both too tired to bring up anything going on between us. Being so tired, it was the fastest I've gone to sleep all week.

I still need to talk to Dean about what happened. There need to be boundaries, clear and cut. That kiss was uncalled for. I was upset and vulnerable, and Dean crossed the line. How could he think that that was the best thing to do in that moment?

Pulling my hoodie farther over my face, I wonder when things will get back to normal and we can work out indoors again. Despite the weather, I've been spending a lot of time outdoors. After Emma's memorial on Friday, I managed to get a minor drug dealer in the Ashland neighborhood arrested—someone who was originally hired by Bello. That was a long and cold night. Much like this morning.

Not going to the gym with Dean will help drive my point home. He needs to understand that he can't ever cross that line again. I just can't figure out how to bring it up. I'm still too mixed up about everything. Emma's funeral was two days ago. I can barely wrap my head around that.

In an attempt to pull myself out of my head, I focus on my breathing as I jog. The clinic is farther than I anticipated, and I feel like I'm dying by the time I finish my run. It's not until I get to the parking lot that I remember that even Dean thought running from my apartment to the clinic was too far.

The lights are off in the clinic, but Alex's car is outside so I knock. She seemed upset the last time I used the alarm code to let myself in. I see her head peek through the small window at the top of the door before she opens it.

"Ethan, what are you doing here so early?" She pulls me inside and relocks the door behind me. "Look at you, you're freezing!"

I wipe the dribble from under my nose with my sleeve. "I'm fine." The rain was a good way to wake me up, but now I'm ready for a hot shower.

"Is this your new training regimen now that you've cut Dean loose?" she asks as she leads me to a closet where she pulls out a towel and a hospital gown. "Put this on. At least you'll be dry."

I've avoided talking to her about Dean, for all sorts of

reasons. Taking the towel, I say, "I'll be fine."

She rolls her eyes and heads back to her office, and I follow.

"So how have you been, really?" she says. "I'm sorry I couldn't make it to the funeral, by the way. I had to work."

I nod and lean on the doorway to her small office. It's cluttered with papers and coffee cups and wrappers. There are two chairs, but one is stacked with books.

"It's okay. Thanks for coming to the wake."

"Of course. Wes wanted to come too, but one of us had to be here." Her former professor at Olympia University helped design the suit I wear during my midnight strolls. Fuse, as I've been called.

"Right, I understand."

"We were listening through the com when it happened. Didn't hear much, just lots of screa—"

"Alex," I cut in, "I'd rather not talk about it."

"Oh. Sorry." She tucks her hands between her knees and stretches out her legs.

Nobody knows what to say to me anymore. This last month and a half has changed me—and I don't just mean the lightning strike that altered the genetic makeup of my body and gave me the power to shoot lightning out of my fingertips. Although I once thought otherwise, that's something I can learn to live with.

Mostly I feel like I've changed for the worse. Lying, sneaking around, being distant. I used to think of myself as a good friend and someone who's generally fun to be around. Since Emma and I witnessed that drive-by, though, my life has gotten considerably darker. I don't like it.

Alex breaks into my thoughts. "So what happened between you and Dean, then?"

"What do you mean?" My heart rate quickens.

"Well, I haven't really talked to you since Detective Cross and I told you about him last week. You seemed pretty upset."

I was furious when I left. But then everything with Bello happened and I was too wrapped up in losing Emma. And then the kiss…

"I haven't talked to him about it yet."

She lifts her eyebrows. "Ethan, it's been almost a week. Is he still staying with you?"

I shrug.

"Ethan!"

"What do you expect me to do? Kick him out on the street?"

"He's a *criminal*!"

"His *family* are criminals. That arrest report was from years ago. He doesn't do that stuff anymore." I'm not positive about that, but I'm pretty certain. Still, I'd be lying if I said the suspicion hasn't crept into my mind.

She lets out a huff of air and rubs the back of her neck behind her hair. "Okay."

I cross my arms. "What?"

"Nothing."

"No, tell me. I want to know."

"You're different. And not in a good way. Even when you were laid up in the hospital, you had a good head on your shoulders. You even had a sense of humor. But since you started going to PT…"

"You mean ever since *you* recommended Dean to me," I clarify.

"Whether he's influencing you to be a bad person or not, the fact of the matter is you are who you surround yourself with," she continues. "You *know* Dean's not a good person, so I don't understand why you haven't distanced yourself from him."

"Because he's my friend!" I stop myself from yelling further. My need to protect Dean is surprising. Like a reflex, but I can't let Alex or anyone else tell me he's a bad person. He saved me. Helped prepare me to face Bello. Despite everything, he's a good friend.

"Last I checked, I've done some pretty bad things too," I continue. "It's called circumstance. Contrary to what you may think, Dean *is* a good person. If you don't believe me, just listen to the com recording from last week. He showed up, fought off friends of the Martellis, and saved me. Would he have done that if he was still in bed with them?"

"You probably could've gotten out on your own."

"In a body bag? Sure. Besides, I thought you hated the idea of me being Fuse."

She studies me. "No, I'm not a huge fan of it. But I can't argue with results. It was because of you—"

"And Dean," I add.

She glares at me. "You helped put Bello away. If you had just stood by, he would've continued doing all the illegal activities he was doing."

"He's not the only one."

Sighing, she says, "I know."

"Which means I have more work to do."

"You need to be more careful."

"I'll need Dean's help."

She rolls her eyes.

"He's the only one who's been on the inside and knows the way they operate. Sure, the police have been watching the Martellis, but they have to follow protocols. Fuse can bend the rules."

"Talking in the third person now?"

Ignoring her, I continue. "Dean's been working with me. Training me. Teaching me who's who in their system. He's essential to my success."

She crosses her arms and stares at me. "Ethan, just please be careful."

"I'll do my best."

Chapter Three

Stretching my legs out on the bathroom floor, I apply a disinfectant to both of my knees. I slipped up last night—quite literally—and skinned both my knees. I was chasing after Victor Vance, a gang leader who used to answer to Bello.

I wanted to put away the rest of the guys in Bello's operation, but thanks to the city's neglect of Hopman, I tripped on the cracked sidewalk and went down hard on my knees. Nothing too terrible, but it took off a layer of skin and made my knees sore for the rest of the night. After I chased down Vance and called him in, I turned in for the night. Luckily, Dean and Cale were both asleep when I came home, so they didn't see my limp.

Once I have a large bandage on each knee, I use the edge of the bathtub to help myself up and then stagger into the kitchen. Running this morning surprisingly didn't hurt, but my knees still tighten up if I sit too long. I'm sure I could ask Dean for some stretches to do.

Plopping down at the kitchen counter, I let out a deep breath as I look down at Frank Rizzoli's card in one hand and my phone in the other. Cale was right. I do need to get a job after getting fired from Wyatt Industries last week for taking time off—without permission—after Emma's attack. Meaning my last paycheck from Wyatt is coming soon and then I have nothing left.

But if all goes well with Frank Rizzoli's offer to work at Tranidek Energy, my unemployment may be short lived.

I rap my knuckles against the granite, stalling. Rizzoli's a high-ranking member of the Martelli family, and Dean says he's dangerous. But I don't have any other job offers. This is the best option for me right now. I have to at least see where it goes. Besides, I'm not making any headway dealing with my thoughts on Dean. Or letting go of Emma. Getting a job will—if nothing else—get my mind off of things for eight hours a day.

His secretary is reluctant to put me through to him, but I tell her my name and insist that I talk to him directly, hoping I don't upset him.

"Mr. Pierce!" he says happily when the call waiting music stops. "I was beginning to think I'd never hear from you again."

"Yeah, sorry. Last week was, uh…"

"Oh, I heard. So sorry about your friend."

Should I bring up the fact that Carlo Martelli told him to offer me a position? Is that really what I want to talk about right now? Would he even talk about that over the phone? Nope, let's keep this conversation on track.

"Thanks. Listen, I was wondering if I could come in and talk to you about that position—if it's still available, that is." I pace the room and run my sweaty hands through my hair. I haven't showered yet, so my hair is matted and I'm still in my gym shorts from my run this morning.

"Oh, sure. Uh, let me check my schedule here…"

Taking this job would be walking into the lion's den, I know that. Carlo Martelli wants to keep me close and under a watchful eye. What I don't understand is why. Dean doesn't think I should allow myself into the snares of the crime family—*his* family. But faced with unemployment and the horrible job market in the city, I don't have any other choice. Besides, at a time in my life when so much is happening *to* me, moving forward with this job is a small way of taking control right now. And, the way I see it, having an ordinary job will help throw off suspicion that I'm Fuse.

"Let's see, I have some time tomorrow afternoon. Say, two o'clock?"

"Uh, yeah," I say, pretending to check my calendar, "that works for me." My heart rate quickens. I didn't think the meeting would be so soon. I have to update my résumé, iron my suit, put together my references…

"Okay, I'll mark you down. See you then, Mr. Pierce."

"Thanks."

Ending the call, I breathe a sigh of relief. The potential for a job is still there. Once I secure it, then I'll tell Cale. He'll be thrilled. Still, I wonder: Despite Carlo's influence, would Rizzoli be keen on giving me a job if he knew that I was fired from my last one?

Actually, I'm more concerned about Dean. He'll probably try to talk me out of accepting the job, but in a way, my unemployment affects him as well since he's been my newest roommate. No job, no apartment, no place for Dean to live, either.

In an effort to pull off all the Band-Aids in my life, I call him up too. I've put off talking to him for long enough. A part of me wonders if I would've been able to put away *more* petty criminals this week if he'd been helping me. Either way, it's time we mend fences. The least I can do is just ignore what happened between us and pretend everything is okay. Reset our relationship to what it was before. That starts with a favor.

My heart pounds in my chest as the phone rings, and I begin pacing again. Hopefully he has a minute in between patients to take my call.

I shake my head. When did I start getting nervous about talking to Dean?

"Ethan, what's wrong?"

"Nothing, I just wanted to talk to you about something. Do you have a minute?"

"Uh, sure. You couldn't have waited until tonight?"

"No, it's about Cale. He might be home later."

"Oh."

Chapter Three

"He has his meeting with Leon Wallace tonight. I want to check in on him to make sure nothing happens."

"So watch him," Dean tells me.

"I want you to come with me."

"Why? You've been running around town just fine on your own." I can hear the bitterness in his voice. "You can handle a simple observation."

I guess I haven't been sneaking out as well as I thought. Since Dean's crashing on the couch, it's kind of impossible to leave without him noticing. But I've been efficient. I'm responsible for a few drug dealers and gang members' arrests. By the sounds of it, Dean's jealous. Feels excluded, probably. I can't really blame him.

I let out a deep breath as I swallow my pride. This is the moment where I put my money where my mouth is and prove that I meant what I said to Alex yesterday.

"I want you there. We're a team. This last week without you I've realized that." Absentmindedly, I smooth out the edges of my bandages.

He's silent and my mind floods with thoughts. Is he mad? Upset? Is he going to punish me for me shutting him out last week? Am I being ridiculous for thinking things can just go back to the way they were?

"Okay," he says with a sigh. "I'll come."

Instantly, my body feels lighter. I close my eyes and smile, thankful that he can't see my reaction. "Thank you."

"What time?"

"His meeting's at six at Wallace's office downtown." Snatched that bit of information from Cale's phone while he was in the shower this morning.

"What's the plan?"

"I don't know yet. That's what I'm going to figure out today." As if I need more things to do.

"Okay."

His short responses are enough to tell me that he's annoyed. I don't really blame him. I've been distant, especially with him. But he has to know this isn't an easy time for me. Each day is a challenge to get out of bed, knowing that I'm the reason Emma's gone. It's hard enough to keep myself going, let alone worry about someone else.

But I suppose I need to figure out some way to work Dean back into my life. My scraped knees are proof that I need him. I just don't know what our relationship looks like going forward. For now, this is the easiest step for me.

———

DEAN AND I are perched on the roof of the Stanley, an historic hotel right on South Main Street downtown. Across Clinton Street to the south is the three-story building that houses Leon Wallace's office. Very modest compared to the towering buildings surrounding it, but since this is part of the historic district, these buildings have been saved from demolition.

Despite being several floors up from Wallace's office, Dean and I have a decent vantage point into his window. We can see Wallace sitting at his desk and Cale sitting opposite. We watched my brother enter from the street. We're only a few blocks away from Myra's apartment, which is where he came from.

Their conversation seems to be polite. Rather mild, actually, considering the accusations Cale is likely insinuating. Just as long as my brother comes back out of the building and makes it safely to wherever it is he's going, that's all that matters for tonight.

Pulling the binoculars away from my face, I lean back and look over at Dean.

"We need to get you more stealthy attire." He's wearing a black sweatshirt with the hood up and dark jeans, but compared to the jet-black Fuse suit, he's more noticeable.

"You're assuming this is going to be a regular thing." He keeps his eyes on Wallace's building.

"Well, are we really done? Bello might've been arrested, but that doesn't mean his operation has completely stopped. Besides, he and his men saw me without my mask."

"Without someone in the family protecting them, the pimps

and drug dealers aren't even going to try to continue business-as-usual. My father will make sure of that. And nobody is going to take Bello seriously in prison if he says you're Fuse."

I turn back to Wallace's building, glad that the mask is hiding my face. My chest burns, and I debate whether I should bring up his father. Tonight is our first step back to normalcy. Is it too soon to discuss the tension between us?

"What's going on with your apartment? It's been awhile since you've been able to stay there." I try to keep the suspicion from my voice. A part of me still wonders whether Dean's just a spy for his father, working his way into my life to make sure I don't expose any of their secrets.

Of course, that's probably Rizzoli's job too, but I imagine Carlo Martelli likes to be thorough.

Dean shrugs. "I don't know. I probably should check it out, though. If it's still being watched, I'm moving out. I can't keep paying for a place I don't even live in."

True. He's been staying with me and Cale for a couple weeks now, sleeping on our couch. It's not ideal, but it's better than worrying about someone breaking down your door in the middle of the night to kill you. Not that I know *why* Dean's place was being watched.

"We should go soon," Dean continues. "Probably during the daytime, just in case."

I smile, although I know he can't see it. We really are getting back to normal. Maybe that kiss can just be put behind us. "Want to go tomorrow on your lunch break?"

He nods. "Sure, sounds like a plan."

Looking back to Wallace's window, I make sure that he and Cale are still engaged in what appears to be a civil conversation. My nerves are still strung out, but keeping an eye on the people I care about is helping. I can't be too careful with Martelli or his men. With Dean by my side, it proves my caution is justified.

"So…we should probably talk about your family sometime," I start.

"I guess so."

"Why didn't you tell me that you're a Martelli?"

"Ethan, up until three weeks ago, you were just my patient. Everything's happened so fast. Besides, it's not like you were completely honest with me about this." He indicates my suit.

"I was once you found out."

"Just the same way I'm not denying what you know," he counters. "My mom did her best to keep me out of the family business. My father gave up a long time ago on grooming me to take over for him. I'm his only kid, and he saw it as a disgrace that I wanted nothing to do with that. An insult to his name, among other reasons."

"But you were a part of it for a little while, at least." The arrest report with Dean's teenaged face on it flashes in my mind. Definitely not the same person who's sitting beside me now.

He shrugs. "After my mom died, there was no one to fight my battles for me. When she passed, I was lost. Dropped out of school, couldn't keep a job, I had nothing. Getting into the business was my only option."

"What made you decide to leave, then?" I'm not sure how old he is, but he has to be at least my age, maybe a little older. To become a certified physical therapist, he had to have gone through years of schooling—or at the very least, finished high school.

"I got caught." He runs the tip of his finger around the rim of the binoculars. "I wasn't in it long. Three years, maybe. There was this landowner who didn't want to pay my father his stipend. Like a tax my father collected to keep a neighborhood safe and drug free."

"But Bello was selling drugs."

"Not that my father knew. Not until we exposed him last week. Anyway, this guy refused to pay, so me and, uh, Jamie were told to harass this guy. Leave notes, smash his windows, scare him into paying. Whatever it took."

"Jamie?"

"James Alexander."

Right. The man Dean lived with for a while. I still don't know the whole story there, but I decide to let him finish instead of pestering him with more questions.

"I thought a good way to scare him was to confront him. Hide out in his car until he was alone." He shakes his head. "Cop saw me trying to break in, knew the name, and thought punishing the boss's son would be a good way to get at my father. The cop probably thought he struck gold with me and either I would expose my father or he'd come out and confess. That obviously didn't happen."

"Did you go to jail?"

"Just until my trial. Thought my father would help me, but he didn't even visit me. Sent Jamie instead to remind me to uphold *omertà*."

"What's that?"

"A policy to keep your mouth shut, basically."

"Did you?"

He shrugs. "Yeah. Otherwise they would've killed me. Didn't matter that I was his son. I wasn't a high-ranking member of the family. I was useless to him. That's the way my father works."

"Dean, that's horrible." I wrestle with myself, wondering if I should say or do anything else. Instead, I let him continue.

"I think that's why my father's men were watching my apartment a few weeks ago. They must've known I was your therapist. My father has his eyes on everyone. After word spread of the drive-by you saw, they must've discovered the connection and assumed I didn't uphold *omertà*."

"So they were coming to kill you?"

He shrugs. "Maybe. Probably more likely that they just wanted to smack me around a little to scare me."

"Do you think they're still watching?"

Dean shakes his head. "Not as closely. Not after Bello was arrested. They have more pressing things to worry about."

Clearing my throat, I ask, "So after you were arrested, how'd you get out?"

"Well, luckily, the judge didn't share the same thoughts with the cop who arrested me, so he let me go. Said it was my first offense and that I would be watched closer. I was only seventeen. He said he wanted to see me become more than just my name."

"And?"

"It worked. Got my GED, then went off to college."

"How'd you get out of the family business? I thought people were never allowed out of the mafia?"

He shakes his head. "Not usually, no. I played my father's game and went to him like a man. Told him how I upheld *omertà* and reminded him of how much my mother would've hated to see me working for him. He said that as long as I stayed in Olympia and continued to be loyal to the family—kept their secrets, basically— he would keep me out of the business."

Dean was out. He was safe. He had the life he worked for.

"Until me." I stare at my gloved hands in my lap.

"You're different."

I glance across the street into Wallace's window. They're still talking. It's been awhile. I wonder if Cale finally broke Wallace, but my mind soon drifts back to Dean. "I'm sorry I've been an ass this week."

"Don't apologize for that. I get it. Your girlfriend just died. You just got fired. Your life is a mess."

No need to sugarcoat it, then.

"Yeah."

Another long pause, then he asks, "Are we going to talk about the other night? When I, uh, kissed you?"

I keep my eyes on the window across the street. We should talk about it. I know. I just haven't figured out what it meant yet. Not to me—still dealing with everything I felt for Emma—and not what that means with Dean. Why did he do it? I suppose the only way to find out is to ask him, but I'm afraid of what he'll say. Afraid of how things will change.

But things have already changed between us.

"Dean, I don't—"

Something catches my eye in Wallace's office. Movement. I don't see Cale at first, and I start to panic until I spot him in the window next to Wallace's office. He's leaving, but he's alone. Some-one else is in Wallace's office now.

Snatching the binoculars from Dean's hands, I look through the window. I know that guy. He's a minor drug dealer I ran into last week right after Emma died. Same blond hair, same flannel jacket.

Chapter Three

What the hell is he doing meeting Wallace?

I get to my feet and open my mouth to tell Dean that I want to get a closer look, but a woman's scream cuts off my train of thought.

My eyes dart down to the street. She screams again, and I spot her on the corner of Stanley and Clinton.

"Stay here." I throw the binoculars at Dean and run the length of the building. Without thinking, I jump off the edge, then panic as I begin to free fall.

I manage to grab ahold of the fire escape, my body slamming hard into it, and I wince at the pain. Pulling myself up to the landing, I race down the stairs to the street and jog over to the source of the screams.

The woman backs away when she sees me, terrified. This is the first time I'm making such a public appearance as Fuse, but I have to see what she's screaming about.

Propped on the bench with a copy of the *Olympia Tribune* in its hands is a skinless cadaver. One leg is crossed over the other and its arms are propped up, holding the paper as if it were alive.

Despite the horrific site, the front page of the newspaper catches my attention. A large headline is spread across the top of the paper: "Bello accepts deal to expose mafia."

Chapter Four

My head's in a cloud this morning. I barely remember the walk from my apartment to the subway station, and the crowd of people squeezing onto the train car doesn't bother me like it usually does. My eyes stare absently at the advertisements above the windows as the train rolls by with a clatter.

That body last night was not an accident. My first thought, based on the newspaper article, was that the Martelli family had skinned themselves a rat and set him out as a warning to others. But that seems too bold, even for the Martellis. Besides, if my memory is correct, Michael Bello is quite a bit taller than the skinned man. Still I'm not positive. Clearly, it was posed—probably by that guy I saw in Wallace's office—and was meant to be seen and to send a message. But to who? Leon Wallace? Carlo Martelli? City government? It was yesterday's newspaper, so it might just be a way to timestamp the murder, but why?

The location of the body doesn't help me much, either. Being downtown, I wonder what the significance of that spot is. It's right in front of Olympia National Bank, across from the elite

Stanley Hotel, and a block north of the Federal Reserve. Perhaps someone wealthy was meant to see it. Of course, it was also close to city hall and even Wyatt's administration building. Main Street was probably too crowded to prop the body, but Stanley and Clinton Streets aren't exactly barren during the daytime.

The better question is, who is the victim? That might help shine some light on who killed him and why. The likelihood of it being someone the victim knew is high. Skinning someone and planting them like this would take a lot of work and preparation.

The train shifts and the man in front of me stumbles backward onto my foot.

"Sorry," he mutters before returning to his paper.

Glancing over his shoulder, I catch part of the article he's reading. "Body" is displayed at the top of the column, likely continued from the front page. The few lines I catch say something about forensics and the methods police can take to identify the body.

The fact that this has hit the news brings me back to the specifics of last night. Michael Bello is the only one I can think of as a potential victim. At least until I find further evidence. Last night I wasn't able to find much more on him other than the fact that he was given a plea deal to rat out the rest of the Martelli family. I'd say that would be a pretty big target on his back.

I'm so lost in thought that I almost miss my stop, much to the dislike of my fellow commuters, who grumble as I push past them to exit the train before the doors shut me in. It's the tail end of the morning rush hour commute, but still, there are a lot of people trying to squeeze onto the staircase leading to the street.

My meeting with Frank Rizzoli is this afternoon, so I figured I'd stop by the police station this morning to see if I can get any information on the corpse from Tucker. Better to make the most of my unemployment, right? Everyone wants me to get out of the apartment anyway.

Once I get past city hall and the downtown medical campus, most of the walkers fade away. Traffic, however, is backed up since East and West Division Streets at Main Street are closed so crews can install the giant Christmas tree in Main Place Park. In all the madness, I almost forgot that Thanksgiving is in two days. It's the first holiday without Emma.

Pushing the thought out of my head, I weave between the cars full of frustrated drivers to the police station. I was hoping Tucker would see me as I came in and would pull me back to his desk, but that's not the case. The whole station seems to be in a frenzy.

"Can I help you?" a woman at the front desk asks after a minute. She sounds annoyed, but judging from the stacks of paper on her desk and the scurrying throughout the office, she must be busy.

"Uh, yeah. I was just hoping to talk to Detective Cross," I say.

"Do you have an appointment?" Her hand hovers over the ringing phone.

"No, I don't. He's a friend of mine and I was just hop—"

Holding up a finger to me, she picks up the phone and says, "Olympia Police Department, please hold." She puts the call on hold and looks up at me. "What's your name?"

"Um, Ethan Pierce."

She indicates a metal chair against the wall. "Have a seat. I'll see if he's got a minute. It could be awhile, though."

"That's okay," I say, but she's already returned to her waiting call.

Taking a seat, I tuck my hands under my knees and consider leaving. He's going to find it highly suspicious that I'm asking about this. Especially after what just happened with those two murder cases I was questioned about, both within a short time of each other. One I was actually guilty of—back when I was still figuring out how to handle my power as Fuse.

And while it's one thing to follow this story in the papers, it's another to come down to the police station asking for information. If Tucker tells Cale, he will probably think it's part of my twisted grieving process or something—because apparently I have nothing else in my life besides missing Emma.

That's it. I'm leaving. This was a mistake. Everyone is clearly very busy. Tucker isn't going to tell me anything anyway.

I stand and turn to leave, but I hear my name.

Chapter Four

"Ethan, what's going on, man?" Tucker shakes my hand and then hooks his thumbs on his belt.

"Are you busy?"

"I'm a little swamped, but I have five minutes. What's up?"

"Uh," I hesitate, but he's right in front of me. Might as well ask what I came here to ask. "Is there any new information on that body that was found last night? The, uh, skinless one?"

Slowly, he shakes his head. "Man, what are you doing?"

Quickly I add, "Just curious. I mean, I read that the body was found with the newspaper announcing Bello's plea deal. I just thought…"

"You just thought the body was Bello? Look, if you're worried about him coming after you next, rest assured that we have it under control. He's not going to hurt you."

"So he's alive?"

He shakes his head. "Snooping around things you shouldn't be is only going to get you in trouble. Look what's happened to you already."

I shrug. "I know. I just thought…"

"Ethan, you've been through a lot. I know you're probably just trying to distract yourself, but this is dangerous. Read about it in the papers, man."

I nod wordlessly.

He puts one of his big hands on my shoulder. "It's a tough time, I know, but focus on the friends and family you still have and you'll come out on the other side."

"Thanks."

He returns his hand to his hip. "What about that Dean kid? What ever happened with him?"

"Uh, well, right after you guys told me is when…that was the night Emma—"

"Word of advice? Lay low and stay away from that guy. Nothing good is going to come from him."

"Hey, is Alex here?" I ask as I lean in the doorway of the small office at the clinic.

Wes has a stack of folders in his lap and he's leaning over, typing on the computer when I walk up. "Not today. It's her day off. What's up? Anything I can help you with?" He shoots me a quick look but keeps typing.

I wanted to ask Alex's opinion on the body, from a medical standpoint. I want to chase down any lead I can. Wes, however, is still a doctor, even if his specialty is in mutations.

"Well, you know that body that they found downtown? The one that was, uh, propped up with a newspaper?"

This gets his attention. He looks over at me with wide eyes. "The skinned one?"

I nod. "That's the one."

He sets his stack of folders on the counter and motions toward me. "Come in and shut the door."

I take a seat on the swivel stool he passes in my direction. The room is so small that my back is pressed against the door.

He pulls off his glasses and leans back, studying me. "I take it this has something to do with, um, Fuse?"

Again, I nod. "Yeah. I went out to see one thing and discovered another."

"You *saw* the body?"

"Up close and personal."

"I guess I'm confused, Mr. Pierce, what exactly you would like from me. It seems *I* should be the one asking *you* questions."

I scratch my head as I think. "Well, I wanted to get your professional opinion on it. A corpse like that would have to be dead a couple days, right?"

"Was there blood? The paper, of course, didn't show any photos and didn't offer a lot of insight into the scene of the crime."

I try to remember. I was so engrossed by the fact that I was staring at a body without any skin—and then the headline—that I wasn't paying attention to blood.

I shrug. "I don't really remember. I think so."

"Then if that's the case, I can't imagine they were dead for long. Maybe a couple hours, at most."

"Interesting," I mutter.

"As gruesome as it is, it is quite fascinating. There's the biological perspective and then the psychological perspective—both from the victim, if they were alive during the process, and the killer. What pushed them to treat another human being in that way?"

"I don't know," I reply. And I really don't. Why would someone want to do that to another person?

———

DEAN'S APARTMENT IS only a few blocks from mine in one of the few buildings that still stood after the Wind Tunnel was laid through the center of the city. Funny, because if the highway wasn't there, Dean's building would only be a ten-minute walk from mine.

Once we get to his floor, Dean hesitates before continuing down the hall.

"If there's anyone in there, you zap them," he tells me. "No questions, just zap and run, got it?"

I nod. "We'll see."

He pulls his keys out of his black dress pants as we approach. Slowly, he slides the key into the lock and gently turns it, trying to keep the noise to a minimum.

When he swings open the door, a putrid smell hits us, worse than anything I've experienced before.

"Holy shit, Dean, what did you leave in your fridge?"

He pulls his green polo up to cover his nose. "The smell would be contained if it were in the fridge."

True. Nervously, I make the first step into his apartment. Other than the stench, it's a nice place. It's a studio, so it's small, but the large windows looking out onto the street below let in so much light.

Scanning my eyes from the kitchen area at one end of the room to the bedroom area at the other, I don't see anything too out of the ordinary. Dean, however, approaches the bathroom slowly.

"It's coming from in here." He's got his nose pinched completely now, and his shirt is still pulled up over it.

Pushing open the door, he immediately recoils and bends over coughing and gagging.

"What is it?" I step closer and peer inside. Immediately, I wish I hadn't.

The bathtub is stained red with blood and pieces of flesh are stuck to the floor and vanity. The worst, though, is the bucket swarming with files. Inside is what appears to be skin, bloody and sliced as if someone peeled off a wetsuit.

I bring a hand to my mouth and turn away, willing myself not to vomit.

"Let's get out of here," I suggest, but Dean's already on the other side of the room.

"Look at this." He pulls away the blanket from his bed, revealing knives, hooks, scalpels, even a box of latex gloves.

"Dean, this must be…"

"Where the murderer killed that corpse we found last night, yeah."

I stare at the collection on the bed, wondering who had access to Dean's apartment. More importantly, why would they set up shop in someone else's home? Wouldn't they expect whoever lived here to come back?

Unless they know Dean's been staying with us. In which case, they know who I am. Who Cale is. If it's someone in the Martelli family, then Cale meeting with Leon Wallace was a big mistake.

"You should clear out of here. Take any valuables and then call the police."

He shakes his head. "No, then the murderer will know I came back and saw. Chances are they know who I am. Maybe even where I'm staying."

There's one fear confirmed.

"If we move anything here, that just puts a target on my back."

"And what happens when the neighbors complain about the stench? They're going to look at you, Dean."

Chapter Four

"I'll figure it out then. For now, I just want to get out of here."

I nod. "Good. I'm going to throw up if I stay any longer."

I stand by the door as he re-covers the bed, trying to fix the blanket so it looks like it did before we came. I consider calling the police, but what Dean says still holds true. That'll just put a target on his back because the murderer will still be on the loose.

As we walk away from his apartment as quickly as we can, I try to keep Tucker's warning out of my head.

———

After Dean drops me off at home on his way back to work, I pull up the *Tribune* on my computer and scroll through the headlines. It's quarter to one in the afternoon, and my meeting with Rizzoli is in a little over an hour. I know I should eat something, but after what I just witnessed in Dean's apartment, I'm not sure I'll ever have an appetite again.

It's weird. After seeing the home base for the murder, and after last night's confessions, I feel closer to Dean—as a friend. But what Tucker said to me still rings in my ears. What if he's right and being friends with Dean is the worst thing for me? Alex seemed hesitant about him the other day when I talked to her, too. Maybe I'm just being foolish ignoring all of them. I can't even determine what my gut is telling me anymore.

A new story pops up right as I'm about to give up on finding any news, so I click on it and skim it over. Other than the fact that the body was found, the article is mostly fluff.

"Calls to the Olympia Police Department weren't returned at press time."

"Investigation is still ongoing."

"No further information is known at this time."

Basically, a dead end. Tucker likely won't be much help anymore. At least not for a while. He's worried about me, and without a plausible reason to be asking questions, my interest is suspicious. I'll just have to be more creative with my research, maybe by hacking into the police server.

Glancing at the time, I see it's already one o'clock. I have an hour to shave, shower, and get down to Rizzoli's office. If I'm late, the last hope I have of regaining my life is gone. Dramatic, I know, but it gets me moving.

Forcing myself to switch my mind off, I zip through my showering routine and reach for my fancy suit before I realize it's the same one I wore to Rizzoli's dinner party. I'm afraid it'll give the impression that it's the only one I own. Well, technically it is, but I don't want Rizzoli to know that.

In a frenzy, I grab the nicest shirt I have and a pair of black pants and pull them on. Both probably could use a good ironing, but they'll do in a pinch. I fix myself in the mirror one last time before running out the door.

The trip to Rizzoli's office doesn't take as long as I'd anticipated, and I'm surprised to see Mr. Rizzoli in the outer office when I get up to his floor. He's wearing a deep purple shirt under his gray suit coat, which has a matching pocket square.

"Perfect timing, Mr. Pierce," he says with a smile as he shakes my hand. "I was just coming back from a lunch meeting. Come on in."

Trying to hide how flustered I am, I follow him to his office. Suddenly, I'm incredibly nervous.

"Take a seat," he says, motioning to the sitting area by the window. When the door closes, the world seems to slow down.

"Sorry for taking so long to make a decision," I say. "Last week wasn't an easy one for me."

"Of course. No, I understand." He takes his place across from me. "But, if you don't mind, let's cut the charade. I've spoken with Mr. Martelli, who tells me that you know he told me to offer you the job. To me, because of Martelli, that offer is perpetual unless I'm told otherwise. It's *my* job to justify your position to the board. And, in fact, there *is* a position to fill. But you're the only one it's being offered to."

Gulping, I think of Tucker's warnings only hours before. Dean knows Rizzoli. *He* even warned me about him. And now all pretenses are out the window.

"That's not to say that you're not qualified," he goes on. "On the contrary, once I began looking into you, I was very pleasantly surprised, as I've told you before. So I'm going to make this clear: even though this job offer was instigated by Mr. Martelli, as eternal as the offer may be, your position would be defined by your abilities. I could have fulfilled Martelli's requests by giving you a job in the mail room. But that'd be a missed opportunity, in my opinion. Instead, I want you right in the heart of the company, doing what we do best."

Speechless, I nod.

"Let me also make this clear: this is the last time we will be discussing outside business matters in this office. This floor may be secure, but when you're in this building, you're working for Tranidek Energy."

What other tasks is Martelli expecting of me if I accept this position? Is it a loaded offer? How stupid am I being just sitting in this office right now? Is unemployment the better option?

No. Unemployment means I couldn't afford my apartment. I'd leave Olympia, stop being Fuse, and would give in to the Martellis' attempts to take my life from me.

But working *with* them? I can't do it. If the opportunity for outside business comes up, I'll pass on it. I'm here for a paycheck. If the offers persist, well, I *am* Fuse.

"Understand?" he presses.

I nod. "Absolutely. I agree. I'd honestly like to forget about all that."

Rizzoli smiles. "I'm sure you would. Let's get right into the position, then." He hands me a folder with the Tranidek logo on it. "I already told you about the software you'd be developing, but it's all explained in there. We're on a bit of a deadline, so you'll be jumping right into it and working with the guys downstairs. Probably even on your first day. Training will have to be on-the-job, though I'm certain you won't have trouble adjusting."

I open up the folder and skim through some of the packets. The offered salary jumps out at me. More than I was making at Wyatt.

"Salary, benefits, all the details are explained in there as well," he says. "Like I said before, Mr. Pierce, we're genuinely hoping to have you on board. Take it all home and read through it. The offer may be forever, but I'd encourage an answer soon. We could really use your help on this software so we can rebid the solar streetway project. We'd love it if you could get started as soon as possible."

Closing the folder, I look up at him. Doing what I went to school for *and* making good money at it? I'm sold.

Dean will be nervous about this job. But he's been in my shoes before. Desperate. He knows I have no other choice—not that many other choices could be as good as this.

The fear of working with the Martellis is just that—fear. I've gotten over my fears before. This won't be any different.

If all else fails, I have my alter-ego to fall back on.

"I don't need to think about it anymore," I tell him. "The position sounds great. I accept. Where do I sign?"

Chapter Five

I wrestle with myself the whole way home. Things are starting to look up again. I still miss Emma more than I've ever missed anyone, but getting this job is a step in the right direction. Cale will be thrilled. Myra will want to celebrate. I'll have to catch Mom and Dad up on how I got fired, which will be sugarcoated with my new, better job. I was too afraid to tell them when it happened, and then everything went crazy when I went after Bello.

The person I'm worried about is Dean. He won't be happy I'm working with Rizzoli. And of course he's the only one home when I get back to the apartment.

"Where have you been?" he asks, following me to my room and lingering in the doorway. His shoulders lift as he folds his arms, his eyes taking in my attire.

Kicking off my shoes, I consider lying, but it'd be no use. Where else would I go all dressed up in the middle of the day? "I, uh, had a meeting at Tranidek today."

"Tranidek? You mean with Frank Rizzoli?" His voice rises. "Ethan, I thought I told you how dangerous he was."

I pull off my socks. "And I thought you knew how badly I needed a job."

"So work at another call center or an IT place. Hell, even work at a fucking gas station, but stay away from Frank Rizzoli!"

"You realize people warn me about you too, right?"

"That's different."

Rolling my eyes, I ask, "Besides working with your father, what has Rizzoli done that makes him such a horrible person?"

"Have you considered how the murderer got into my apartment? How they even knew I lived there?"

I shrug. "I don't know. It's probably not that difficult to find someone's address."

"The door wasn't broken into, and I need a key fob to get in the building. It's secure. Any attempt to get in by someone who isn't supposed to be there would raise alarm. Someone let him in."

"Okay, but who?"

"Who do you think?"

I narrow my eyes. "Not Rizzoli. It can't be!"

"I looked into it," Dean pushes. "My apartment building is owned by Corrado Holding Company. Guess who has a significant share in *that* company?"

"So you're saying Frank Rizzoli is the murderer? I don't think someone of his status needs to go around killing people."

"Even if he's not the murderer, he could be the one who let him in or gave him a key or something." He shrugs. "I'm just saying it's a possibility. Meanwhile, you're so quick to jump in bed with him." He cheeks flush. "Never mind."

Unbuttoning my dress shirt, I follow him out to the living room, where he takes a seat on the chair and buries his head in his hands. His knee jumps like a jackhammer.

"Dean, what's going on? You're acting weird."

He rubs his palms on his pants and stares at the wall for a moment. I almost leave the room to change my clothes, but I decide to give him a few more moments. Patience isn't my strong suit, and I need to work on that.

"Sorry," he finally says. "I just thought you wouldn't go to work for Frank Rizzoli. Especially since it's likely he's involved with the murderer." He shakes his head. "You're right. You need this job. You don't need to listen to me anyway."

I let out a breath of air. "I definitely thought about what you said today before I accepted the job. But I need the money. Besides, I'd be doing *exactly* what I've been wanting to do for years. The only thing that kept me at Wyatt so long was Emma, really."

He's quiet, likely giving me time to continue if I want, but I don't. Emma fuels my daydreams, my nighttime dreams, and up until last week, all of my motivations. Now that she's gone, I feel lost. This afternoon was the first step in a new direction. Something that's completely my own. It felt good.

Until I saw Dean's reaction. What is he so afraid of? Does he think I can't take care of myself? Does he think less of me because he had to save me last week from Bello?

I don't voice any of this, though. I *do* need him. Starting an argument is only going to ruin our relationship more.

"Just be careful," he finally says.

I nod. "Of course. Rizzoli is actually the one who told me he's hiring me for my abilities, not because Car—your father—told him to."

Dean clears his throat. "I, uh, actually need to talk to you about that."

"You already told me yesterday. I get it. You're not a part of the family's operations anymore. I believe you." The betrayal I felt last week has passed. Instead, I just feel a little bitter he didn't tell me on his own. But then, I'm the last one who can throw stones.

He shakes his head. "No, not that. I didn't tell you everything."

Heat flashes across my body as I worry what else he could be hiding. Why are there always more secrets? I suppose I shouldn't be one to talk, but by now he knows all of mine. I thought I knew all of his.

Moving over, I sit on the arm of the couch and wait for him to start. His eyes are locked on a spot on the floor a few feet in front of him.

"My father called me yesterday. Before we went out to keep an eye on your brother. I haven't spoken to him since I was eighteen. Nine years ago."

"What does he want?"

"He invited me to Thanksgiving dinner."

"Oh, so it could be harmless then, right?" I hope.

"No. He said when I left the business, I left the family. There were other reasons too, but that was the biggest part. I couldn't call myself a Martelli and live a clean life. That's why I took my mother's name."

"So what do you think he wants, then?"

"I don't know!" He brings a fist to his mouth. "I was trying to tell you last night, but we were talking about other things—things I've been meaning to tell you anyway, and then the body and…" He waves his hand.

The body. That's fallen off my radar since this afternoon. I let it slide again. Right now, Dean's more important.

"He's got me so freaked out. Especially now that we know someone's been in my apartment." He breathes in a shuddering breath.

I stand and step toward him. In my head, I consider if I should hug him, rub his shoulder, something. I wish I didn't have to think about every move I make with him.

"Hey, it'll work out."

"What if it doesn't? You saw what they did to Emma. What if—" He meets my eyes. "What if that happens to you? I can't let it."

My mouth goes dry. Dean's not just worried about being sucked back into the fold. He's genuinely concerned that something's going to happen to me. That he's going to lose me. I wonder if I'd feel the same way if I were in his shoes. I don't know. We come from two different worlds, and I can't even picture being in his situation.

Dean wipes at his nose. "My father wanting you to work for Rizzo means he wants to watch you. Probably suspects that you're Fuse."

I force a smile and let myself rub his muscled shoulder. "So

I'll have to be careful, that's all. I'll be working, so it's not like I'd have to try hard to be careful anyway."

"Yeah," he says absently, still keeping his eyes locked on the floor. His chin is propped up on his hands. "I just hate to see what they've already done to you."

Pulling away from him, my mind goes back to Emma. "Yeah."

"Even before last week. When you first came into my office, you were fired up, feisty, even a little naïve."

He trails off. Only the noise from outside fills the room.

"I was the one who put the note in your office," he confesses.

"What do you mean?"

"Right after you guys saw the drive-by last month."

My eyes narrow as I process what he's saying. "What? How did you know they were watching me? How did you know where I worked?"

"By then you were my patient. I read about the drive-by in the paper, which said that the lightning boy was among the witnesses. I knew my father would want to clean up any loose ends. I couldn't let you walk right into a trap."

"Oh," I say. "I didn't know it was you."

"And now they have you in their sights anyway." He rubs his eyes, facing away from me.

I resume rubbing his shoulder, but it's not enough. I sink onto the cushion next to him and pull him up into a hug, squeezing tighter as his arms wrap around me.

Any paranoia I felt about the kiss or having any sort of physical contact fades away. All I can think about is comforting him. I hate seeing him this upset. Especially if I'm the reason. He's been helping me learn how to defend myself on the streets, but I have more to learn. I need him, and right now he needs me.

This is the first time I've really seen Dean this vulnerable. Even last night, when he told his story, he was so matter-of-fact. Ever since that kiss we've entered a whole new stage of our friendship…or whatever it is.

Friends. That's exactly where I think we ought to be. Where we *should* be. But hugging him, holding him, feels so natural.

Feels right. Easy. Not quite enough.

The room seems to quiet as a warmth in the pit of my stomach rises to my chest. For the first time since I got home, the scent of Dean hits me. I pull away enough to meet his eyes, neither of us saying a word.

Before I have the chance to second-guess myself, our lips are locked once more.

It's different this time. There's more feeling, less confusion. Almost a hunger behind it.

Most surprising of all, I feel the hunger in me.

Finally, my senses return and I pull away. Our chests heave as we stare at each other. I pull my eyes away from him, even though I can still feel his boring into me.

"That was unexpected," he says, with a hint of a smile to his voice.

His reaction makes me angry. Why did I do that? We were just getting back to the way things were and I ruined it.

"Just drop it." I turn to walk back to my room, but he grabs my arm.

"Wait a minute."

I force myself to look at him, telling myself that kissing him was bad. Resisting any urge to do it again. Hating myself for wanting to.

"Can we talk about it? This is the second time—"

"There's nothing to talk about." I pull my arm free from his grasp. "Just leave it alone. Forget it ever happened." I leave the room, but he follows.

"Ethan, after the first time I thought I freaked you out," he presses.

I pull off my dress shirt and swing open my closet door, trying to create as much noise as possible.

"It was bad timing the first time because of Emma, so I let it go," he says. "Now I don't know what to think."

At the mention of Emma, my anger intensifies. Even though I know I shouldn't, I aim it at Dean.

"Awful convenient, isn't it?"

His brow scrunches. "What is?"

Chapter Five

"Emma dies and you move right in. What, were you just waiting for her to die? Thought that once she was out of the way I'd come running to you? Or maybe you just thought that once she was out of the picture I would discover my latent homosexual feelings and fall in love with the first meathead I saw. That's not what's happening here."

My words spill out as my self-control goes out the window. I know I'm getting carried away with my accusations, but I just need everything to stop. I'm angry, and Dean's the easiest target.

He looks defensive. Both of us are breathing heavily for different reasons now.

"Okay, first of all," he starts, "I was never waiting for Emma to die. I thought you had more respect for me than to accuse me of that. Or did you forget that I was telling you that she'd recover? We all thought she would. And second, that kiss last week was my mistake. Up until a few minutes ago, I didn't think you had any 'homosexual feelings.' Based on your reaction, though, I'd say you have some shit to sort out."

My mind runs blank for a retort, so I say, "Fuck you."

"No, fuck you," he fires back. "You're going through a lot, I get that, but don't take it out on me. *You* were the one who just kissed *me*. You're just freaking out because you liked it and it scares you."

"Stop trying to find meaning behind it," I say forcefully. "I was—I thought it'd cheer you up." I'm sure my face is flush with embarrassment. But I'm not sure I can deny what he's saying, which only makes me angrier.

"You thought—" The sound of keys in the door stop him. Moments later, Cale walks in.

"Hello?" When he appears in my doorway, he says, "Hey guys." His eyes jump from me to Dean and back again. We both glare at him. The tension in the room is evident. "Did I interrupt something?"

"No," I say before Dean has a chance to. I brush past my brother to take a shower, resisting the urge to slam the bathroom door for effect.

What was I thinking, kissing Dean? I wasn't, that's the

problem. I just hated seeing him so torn up over everything with his father. And me. I was just being a friend.

I try not to think about his theory that I'm just scared, but it's the thing that seems to stick with me. He has a point. I am scared. Of moving on from Emma. Of letting my guard down. Of liking Dean.

No. Kissing him was wrong and it can't ever happen again. I'm just desperate to fill the hole left behind by Emma. I'm lonely. That part of me should still be reserved for her.

Besides, Dean's a guy. He's not even my type.

———

I NEEDED TO get out of the apartment. The tension between me and Dean would've been too noticeable in front of Cale. The last thing I want is for my brother to know that I've kissed Dean. Twice.

Instead, I'm at 71 Brendan Avenue, also known as the legal address of Gary Todd, the drug dealer I spotted at Wallace's office just before the body was found.

Since I didn't get any real answer out of Tucker or the paper, I've decided to follow my hunch and figure out whether Todd did plant the body and, if so, why.

His neighborhood is just west of Hopman, on the other side of the Wind Tunnel. Todd's house is one of the nicer ones on the street, which still isn't saying much. The paint is peeling outside, there's a busted step on the front porch, and a large cracked window on the side of the house is patched with duct tape.

Just like I did at Aiden Lipinski's house, I creep around to the back. This time, though, I don't have Dean waiting with a quick getaway. The backyard is even worse than the front. It's a small forest of tall grass and forgotten pieces of furniture—an old couch, lawn chairs, a rusted basketball hoop, even a car door.

The backdoor is unlocked and when I step inside, I see the house is nearly empty. Whitewashed walls, cheap countertops, and a fridge that's probably fifty years old are crammed into the tiny galley kitchen. Through the doorway I see Todd spread out on the couch with a beer in his hand, watching TV. He's facing the other way, completely unaware that I'm in the room.

Summoning the electrical charges in my body, I shoot a quick streak of lightning at the TV, and the room goes dark. I run to the couch and grab Todd by the shirt as he's scrambling to his feet.

"Where were you last night?"

"What are you talking—who are you?"

I push him up against the wall and mutter through clenched teeth. "Where. Were. You. Last. Night?"

"I, uh, had a meeting. Yeah. I had a meeting downtown."

"With Leon Wallace?"

"What, are you following me, man?"

I pull him away just to slam him against the wall again. "You dropped that body, didn't you? Did Wallace put you up to it?"

His face scrunches in confusion. "The body—what—are you talking about that skinned one? Man, that's some fucked up shit. I ain't killed no one."

Breathing heavily, I try to determine if he's lying.

"What were you meeting Wallace about?"

"That's classified."

I throw him to the floor. "Not to me it isn't."

Sparks zaps between my fingers.

Todd holds up his hand toward me. "Easy, man, easy. I ain't lying! I took the train downtown, went right to Wallace's office, and I was there for an hour. We heard the screams, saw the police, but stayed inside to avoid it all. Check with Wallace, check the cameras, check the fucking train schedule if you want. I'm telling you, it wasn't me."

My chest heaves as I study him. It makes sense. A scrawny guy like this wouldn't be able to haul a body downtown by himself. Especially not without getting covered in blood. From what I saw through the window last night, there wasn't a spot of blood on him.

Leaning down, I mutter, "Don't tell anyone I was here."

Chapter Six

The line is short at the Buzzing Bar, so I stand back as I read the menu items above the counter. Only five sandwich options, two soup specials, and a small selection of baked goods. Clearly, coffee is their specialty.

The cafe is right across from city hall, on the ground floor of Wyatt's administration building. I haven't been back here since Emma and I first tried it out, back in September when it opened.

I feel a hand on my back and my reflexes kick in. I stop my fist just before it collides with Myra's face.

"Whoa!" she yelps.

Dropping my arm to my side, realizing everyone in the cafe is watching me, I blush. "Oh shit, I'm sorry!"

"Jumpy, are we? You almost broke my nose!" She looks worried, but lets out a nervous giggle.

"I'm so sorry! Please don't tell Cale." He would kill me if he knew I almost knocked out his girlfriend. He's probably also not that fond of the fact that we have lunch frequently, but he hasn't said anything, so I could just be overreacting. It wouldn't be the first time.

She smiles. "I won't, but just relax a little. You don't want to hurt someone."

I nod and we shuffle up to the counter to order.

Since asking Tucker for help with the corpse yesterday was worthless and my number one suspect has been ruled out, I decide to try asking Myra if she has any insight. It's a long shot—namely because it didn't happen in her district—but it's the only other lead I have. There hasn't been anything new in the *Tribune* since yesterday's fluff piece, and Cale isn't working on the story so he doesn't know any more than I do. I'm afraid the trail is going to get cold.

Once we have our food and are seated by the window, she asks, "So what have you been doing that knocking someone out is second nature?"

"Oh, I got that from Dean. The usual gym workouts get boring, so we switch it up." Yeah, that seems like a convincing enough story.

Bringing him up in conversation reminds me of last night. All I did was make things worse. The guilt of it sits like a rock in my stomach. Specifically, those accusations that hadn't even crossed my mind until the heat of the moment. I really wish I hadn't said all that.

"Well, I gotta say, that makes me feel a little relieved that you know *something* about defending yourself now. Especially with everything that's happened to you lately. Did Cale tell you what he saw the other day?"

"Yeah, he texted me. It's crazy what's going on in this city."

She shivers. "Disgusting."

"Did they ever find out who the victim was or who put the body there?"

Shaking her head, she says, "I don't know."

"I just thought you might've heard something around city hall." I pick off some of the extra toppings from my sub.

"Ha! Like I have any time to read into stuff like that! This is the first lunch break I've taken all week."

"It's only your third day on the job. I thought you were mostly keeping things status quo until his replacement got in there."

"Well," she covers her mouth with her hand as she finishes chewing, "Lloyd getting fired ignited paranoia throughout city hall that nobody was safe and that we're all working for the Martellis, which is most definitely not true. So I've been busy doing damage control with the press and trying to sort out the mess he made."

"Oh, that sucks. Whatever happened to the other people at city hall you thought were involved with the family?"

"Well, I *did* find evidence against a few other officials, but finding something that'll hold up in court requires some digging. The case I had going against Frank Lloyd was brought to my attention because I was working with him."

"That makes sense." I take another bite of my sandwich.

"It was also to protect myself, because if I wasn't the one to call out Lloyd on his shady dealings, someone else might've, and probably would've assumed that I was involved too."

"Yeah, then you never would've been named councilwoman—no matter how temporary."

"Exactly." She reaches for her cup and takes a sip.

"So have you looked into the other cases?"

She shakes her head. "Haven't had the time. After they made me Lloyd's temporary replacement, I got so busy with everything. Plus I've been trying to do as much as I can for my district while I have the authority to do it."

"Like what?" I ask around a mouthful. I grab a napkin and wipe the corners of my mouth.

"Well, that's the thing. Next Monday the council is going to announce the special election for the open council position. I thought I could use this time as interim councilwoman to propose programs and put together community events to show that I've taken huge steps in improving the district. It'll be leaps and bounds to what Lloyd did his entire tenure."

"And it's not like there's someone in Hopman organizing their own events to bring back the neighborhood," I add. "You're sure to win."

She smiles again. "Thanks, but I have to be sure. I've been sorting through financial statements and grant applications to figure out where I can get funding for some of these programs. I've already contacted the Baptist church in the center of Hopman about organizing a Christmas parade. I feel like reinvigorating the neighborhood starts with building up community morale."

I lick a drip of mayo from my pinky. "Any luck so far?"

She scrunches up her face. "Eh. The minister said she'd look into it, but she's concerned about the safety of her congregants."

"I don't blame her."

"Me neither, but I need to start getting the residents and the few business owners on board in order to do anything. I can't justify throwing money in a neighborhood that's not even active." She sighs. "It's a bit of a chicken and egg problem."

"I can see that. You'll figure it out, though. I'm sure you could talk to my friend Alex. She might be willing to help in some way." She's the only one I know who has a business in Hopman. Alex and her clinic are the only reason I ever go down to that neighborhood.

Well, that used to be the only reason. Fuse has had plenty of reasons to go down there the last couple weeks. I'm needed down there when I'm behind a mask.

"Oh yeah! I almost forgot she has the clinic down there!" Myra pulls out her phone and pokes at it with her finger. "Give me her name and the number for the clinic so I can get in touch with her."

After I recite Alex's information, I ask, "Isn't this a little out of your job description?"

"It is," she confesses, "but somebody needs to start putting programs like these together. Hopman is where I grew up before it got too bad. I really hate to see what it's become."

"Well, at least Hopman has one thing going for it: someone to fight for it."

She smiles as she slips her phone back in her purse. "Thanks. What about you? Any luck on the job front?"

"Actually, yeah. I accepted a job at Tranidek yesterday."

Her face lights up as she smiles even wider. "Ethan, that's great!"

I grin. "Yeah, I'm excited. It'll definitely be a relief not have to worry about the bills anymore. I know the last few months have been rough on Cale."

"He just wants the best for you. He must be thrilled. What did he say when you told him?"

"Um…I haven't told him yet."

"Why not? He wasn't at my place last night so he *better* have been home." She smirks.

I nod, thinking back to the argument Dean and I had yesterday. "He was, yeah. I just didn't get a chance to."

"Well, I'll save that moment for you. He really is going to be so happy."

He will be, I know that. But my mood is still dampened by everything else in my life. The new job is helping, but it doesn't solve all of my problems.

Then again, what am I complaining about? Myra, Cale, Dean, even Alex and Wes all have problems. Everyone does. They're all working through them and doing their best. I need to be able to do the same.

———

TODAY IS THE first day since everything happened last week that I'm really pushing myself at the gym. I've been running every day, but haven't had the energy to do much else. I'd still rather be at home, but I think by now it's more out of laziness than sadness. I'm determined to get back to the progress I was seeing in my body before.

But what a difference a week makes. The treadmill is a piece of cake. Easier, even, since I'm not breathing in the cold November air like I have been on my runs. The weights, though—that's a different story.

With each machine I try, I need to drop the weight down from what I'm used to. Luckily, the gym is mostly empty so no one sees me struggling. It's embarrassing to pick up a set of weights thinking I can use them the way I did two weeks ago, only to have my muscles strain as I try to lift them.

The worst part is that I'm not sure how much this is helping me. Getting stronger is always a good idea, sure, but when I was working out with Dean, he was showing me how to fight. How to anticipate someone else's moves. How to determine their weak spots. It's how I almost knocked out Myra today.

Breathing heavily, I take a big sip of water while I rest between sets. It's harder to motivate myself without Dean. What I told Alex was true. I do need him. I thought I was just spewing words then, but he's been an integral part of my progress since I met him. Avoiding him this last week has made me even more sure of that. But everything is still so confusing. As I stare in the mirror, I don't quite recognize myself. Why did I kiss him last night? Did the idea just come in my head because he kissed me first last week? Am I gay because of it? Am I a different person than I thought I was?

It might all be a moot point after what I accused him of yesterday. I wouldn't be surprised to find him gone when I get home. I'm reluctant to admit that I'd miss him, but I know I would. And I don't know what that means.

The kiss scares me more than getting struck by lightning did. Both changed me. Both come with their own set of consequences. Neither were expected. The only difference is, with the lightning strike, I had people to help guide me down the road to recovery. With Dean it's just a gray area, and I have no one to talk to about it.

I push those thoughts from my mind and move on to my next set. Worrying about everything with Dean is only stressing me out, and frankly, it's the least of my problems at the moment.

My talk with Myra was good, but the lack of any information about the skinned body was frustrating. I just seem to keep running into dead ends on this case. I have a couple more options, but I'm afraid to use them. I need to be careful to protect my connection with Fuse. Of course, I also need to learn how to be a better Fuse.

After the gym, I circle my way up to the building across from Dean's apartment. The sun is setting, so maybe I can get a decent view inside. *If* there's anyone inside and *if* they have the light on. I have my doubts. With my gym bag strapped to my back, I climb up the fire escape, cursing myself for doing this now with my tired muscles.

I don't even need my binoculars, and frankly, I think it would draw more attention to me anyway. There are several windows with lights on. The whole third floor, actually, including Dean's apartment.

Pulling my sleeves over my hands to keep them warm, I crouch down to block the wind and wait to see movement. Maybe it's a fluke. Maybe we just forgot to turn the light off when we left.

I see a figure cross in front of a window, and I spring into action. Racing down the fire escape and around to Dean's building, I manage to catch the door just as another resident comes out. I run up the steps two at a time, my legs really burning now.

My body slams against the door to Dean's apartment, but it's locked. I consider kicking it in, but that would show that I was here.

Instead, I pound my fist against the door and bellow in a deep voice, "Open up!"

Nothing.

I try again, letting out my frustration with each bang, but still no one answers. Pressing my ear against the door, I listen for anyone inside, but all I hear is a mother down the hall yelling at her kids.

Breathing heavily, I review my options. I can keep slamming myself against the door, but what good is it doing? Whoever is inside knows I'm here, and if they don't answer, it just looks like I'm trying to break in. With one last kick at the door, I slowly make my way back down to the street. Going down the stairs hurts even more than coming up did. Maybe I overdid the leg press.

Before I head back home, I look up to Dean's window and see the light is off. Either whoever I saw is hiding with the lights off or I passed them on my way up. I wonder if it was the person I blew past on my way in, but I barely even looked at them, so that's no help.

It doesn't matter. It just proves that someone is using Dean's apartment. I'm determined to find out who.

———

THE WHOLE WAY home passes in a haze. My mind is still too preoccupied with who was in that apartment, questions about Dean, and ways I can help Myra get elected.

Like a jolt, I stop in my tracks as soon as I walk through the door, though. Cale and Dean are on the couch watching football, each with a beer in their hands.

My brother glances back at me and mutters, "Oh, hey Ethan. Did you go to the gym?"

The answer is obvious because I'm touting my gym bag, but I know it's just my brother's way of keeping track of me. "Yeah."

Dean gets up without looking at me and moves through the kitchen as if he's always lived here. He ducks down to check whatever's in the oven. When the door opens, I smell chicken and garlic and other spices I can't identify.

"Did you know this guy can cook?" Cale asks me, getting up and taking a seat at the counter.

I take the seat next to him. "Yeah, he cooks for me all the time." Well, that made it sound like we're a couple.

Of course, Cale picks up on that.

"Aw, how long have you guys been married? How cute," Cale kids.

"Shut up." The words come out harsh. I meant to play it off as a joke, but my annoyance shines through.

Dean and Cale look at each other but don't say anything. The mood in the room has changed, and we're quiet until Dean declares that dinner's ready. We eat in silence for a few minutes. Since there are only two seats, Dean leans on the counter across from us next to the cooling oven.

"What's this about you ditching me tomorrow for dinner?" Cale starts.

My brows furrows. "What are you talking about?"

"Thanksgiving dinner. Dean says you're going to his family's house."

My stomach drops and the next bite I take has no flavor. I glare at Dean, who gives me a pleading look.

"He's actually going to be working for a, uh, friend of my family's," Dean says quickly.

"Oh, did you get him a job somewhere?" Cale asks him, glancing at me. "Didn't realize you had an interview anywhere. Where was it? That place you were telling me about?"

"Yeah," I say, setting aside my half-eaten plate.

"That's awesome!" Cale slaps my back. "All right, man! Where is it?"

"Tranidek Energy."

"Oh, jumping ship, huh?"

"Yeah."

I can feel Dean watching me. He probably sees that I'm not in a good mood, but I wonder if I'll have a chance to tell him what's really setting me off. How having dinner with his criminal family without my approval is not my idea of a fun holiday.

"It sounds like a great offer," Dean adds for me.

"So what's the job?"

"Uh, software development for the solar roadways. Wyatt's costs are skyrocketing, and Tranidek hopes to step in and finish the work. Or at least split the rest with Wyatt. They want me to help roll out software that'll trump Wyatt's."

"Yeah, Wyatt's stocks aren't doing so hot," Cale says. "And I heard their customer service is subpar." His eyes quickly widen as he remembers that was my department. "No offense."

"It wasn't me. I handled internal calls. The floor below me answered customer calls."

"How much does it pay?" My brother pushes.

"More than Wyatt."

"Really!" His eyes light up. "That's awesome!"

Finally, a smile cracks across my face. Cale is genuinely happy for me. A stark contrast from the scolding he gave me when I got fired from Wyatt. This is just the reaction I was expecting, and it feels good to have my brother's approval and to be moving forward again.

"Yeah, I start on Monday."

Cale stands and brings his plate to the sink. "We should go out to celebrate. Maybe this weekend."

"Sure."

"Well as great as this news is, Myra needs my help with some stuff. Cale heads to his room to change out of his work clothes, and Dean and I fall into another tension-filled silence. I get up and squeeze behind him to rinse my plate. Before I have a chance to figure out whether to avoid Dean or wait for Cale to leave, my brother emerges from his bedroom. He pulls on his coat, slips his wallet into the inside pocket, and slides on his shoes by the door.

"Thanks for dinner, Dean. Ethan, I'll see you tomorr—wait, no." He looks at me with a serious expression. "You're really not coming to Mom and Dad's?"

I glance over at Dean and then back to my brother. "I guess not. Sorry."

A part of me was kind of hoping to see my parents. Not only to assure them that I'm doing okay after Emma, but to get a taste of simplicity. The kind I had before I developed my Fuse abilities and my world went crazy.

But it's probably better that I don't, anyway. My mother especially would probably insist I take time off. It's not like I can talk to either of them about half of what I'm going through. I tell Cale as much as I can, but even that's not enough. Visiting my parents will only serve as a reminder of how much I've changed in the last few months. Besides, I can see them at Christmas.

"No, it's okay," Cale says. "I might be sneaking out early anyway to go to Myra's mom's house anyway."

"Well, Happy Thanksgiving, then," I say.

He smiles and looks at Dean. "Fill this guy up with lots of turkey and pie." He nods to me. "He needs it."

"Will do." Dean offers a mock salute.

When Cale leaves, the silence returns. After Dean rinses his plate and turns back around, I start talking just to fill the air.

"I saw someone at your place tonight."

His eyes grow large. "You did? Who was it?"

"I don't know. I just saw a shadow from across the street. By time I got up there, the door was locked and the lights were off. Couldn't hear anything. Actually, I couldn't smell anything, either." That thought just occurred to me. "He must've cleaned up…what was left."

"Hmm," he mutters. "You think it's that guy you recognized at Wallace's office?"

Shaking my head, I reply, "No, I had a talk with him last night. He doesn't know anything. About the bodies, at least."

"Oh."

Looking up at him, I ask, "What?"

"Nothing."

"No, what is it?"

"Without us knowing who's squatting at my apartment, I'm thinking I should cancel my lease and get a new place. Maybe farther away from the city this time. Just start over."

My breath catches as I study him. I can't let Dean leave. Not with all this Martelli stuff going on. Or the Emma stuff. Or the Fuse stuff. He can't move out.

"Are you serious?" I finally ask.

"Well, Ethan, clearly it's not very safe here."

"Yeah, but—you can't leave."

"Why not? It'd finally be an escape from all of this."

"Would it, though?" I ask. "Think about it: if you leave, it doesn't mean these people aren't still out here. If they want you, they'll find you. Whether you're in Olympia or in, I don't know, China or something."

He smirks. "True."

"You of all people should know that."

"Yeah."

Cleaning my teeth out with my tongue, I consider how I'm going to bring up the whole Thanksgiving thing. How could Dean just assume that I'd want to have dinner with his family? Especially with a murderer on the loose, who could very well be Michael Bello or someone working for him. Bello is someone

Dean himself used to call Uncle Mike. Someone who has damning information on both me and Dean.

The more I think about it, the more annoyed I get. It's one thing for Dean to put himself in the crosshairs, but why does he need to drag me into it?

"Since when am I going to your house for Thanksgiving dinner? You were just bitching about me working for Rizzoli, but now all of a sudden it's okay if we have dinner with them?"

"My father invited me." He turns again and starts filling up the sink with soapy water.

"What about me? Does he even know you're bringing someone? I don't want to just show up." Especially not in that company.

He keeps his eyes on the plate he's scrubbing. "No, you were…sort of invited."

"Sort of? Dean, I'd appreciate it if you'd at least ask me about these things before telling people I'm going!"

"You're right, I'm sorry. I should've asked. But after what you said last night, you owe me this."

I look down and sigh. "You're right. I'm sorry for what I said last night," I confess. "I'm just—"

"I get it. It's a rough time. I haven't been making it easier." He piles the dishes on a towel beside the sink. "Thank you for apologizing, though. And I'm sorry for…" He trails off as he works at a spot on the oven pan.

Picking up a dish towel, I help him dry. "I'm not sure this dinner is a good idea, though. How could it be? You said it yourself: those people are dangerous."

"I haven't seen 'those people' in nine years. I'm going to be walking into a room full of men who don't trust me. I left, so now I'm an outsider. The only reason I'm still breathing is because my father is. I'm terrified to go there tomorrow. But I have to. You don't tell my father no."

"I would've."

He shakes his head. "But you didn't. My father wanted you to work for Tranidek, and now you are." His eyes remain focused on the sink. "One way or another he gets what he wants."

Fuse: Omertà

I hadn't thought about that. A part of me wants to call Riz-zoli back to tell him I'm not taking the job after all, just so I can show Martelli he can't control me. But I can't. I need the money. And Martelli knows that.

Dean hands me the pan and meets my eyes. "I really need you there."

I study him. He doesn't reach for me or give any indication that he's thinking about the kiss last night. He needs me as a friend. Like we've been for weeks. I can't let him down.

"Okay," I relent. "I'll go."

Chapter Seven

My heart pounds in my chest as Dean and I walk up to the front door of his father's house. It's a large ranch on a small cul-de-sac off the parkways in the west end of the city. The midtown skyline soars in the sky behind the house.

The whole way here I felt so lightheaded that I thought I was going to fall off the back of Dean's bike. Hopefully he realized that was the only reason I was clinging to him so tight.

I've only met his father once, and that was when he warned me to keep my mouth shut about the drive-by shooting—which I did—and yet Emma still died. I suppose, technically, he kept his promise of keeping *me* alive. Technicalities are really what drive men like these.

Of course, Michael Bello is really to blame for Emma's death, and it infuriates me that he will walk free after giving testimony against the Martellis. Luckily, the bruises on my face from his beating have almost faded completely. Hopefully no one will notice.

The bigger question eating me up is what Carlo Martelli thinks of me coming to Thanksgiving dinner. Dean never elaborated on what the rationale is for me coming. Did he say I was a friend? Roommate?

Boyfriend?

"You ready?" Dean asks me just before he rings the bell.

I fuss with my outfit. Adjusting the collar, fixing the cuffs, pulling the suit coat into place. "Yeah," I say with a sigh. "Let's get this over with."

"Thanks again for coming." He waits for my response, but all I offer him is a tight smile. I'm still annoyed that I just found out about this less than twenty-four hours ago.

The large white door swings open, and a man dressed in all black with a red tie answers. I can feel Dean tense up next to me. I suppose he's right. He does need my support.

"Dino," the man says. His dark hair is thinning on the top, which he's attempted to disguise with a bad combover. When he smiles, I make a concerted effort not to react to his yellow teeth.

"James." Dean stares a moment longer and then turns to me. "This is Ethan."

The man offers his hand. "James Alexander. Nice to meet you. Come on in."

He leads us through the house to the sunroom, where a handful of people are seated. Everyone is dressed up, and I'm thankful that Dean insisted I wear a suit. When we enter, everyone's eyes turn to us. I recognize a few faces: Frank Rizzoli, Leon Wallace, and Carlo Martelli himself.

The room is silent until James says, "Dino's arrived, sir."

Carlo stands and faces his son. Dean is nervous, I can tell. He takes in a deep breath, keeps his shoulders back, and stands straight as a board. The others watch quietly, and a few even seem to scowl at us. The tension in the room is evident.

Finally, after what feels like forever, Carlo smiles and says, "My son." He steps forward, grabbing Dean's face in his hands and kissing each cheek before pulling him into a tight embrace. Over Dean's shoulder, he mutters, "My son" over and over again.

When they pull away from each other, Carlo holds Dean's face again and beams. "You look good. Been taking care of yourself, then?"

Dean nods. "Yes, sir."

"Been keeping your mother's name clean, too. I appreciate that."

"Of course."

Carlo pats Dean's arm and then extends his hand to me. "How've you been, Mr. Pierce?"

"Good," I say, giving his hand a firm shake. Then add, "Sir."

Frank Rizzoli steps up and shakes my hand. "Happy Thanksgiving, Mr. Pierce." He indicates Dean with his glass of dark liquor. "I didn't realize you two were…so close."

I nod and force a smile, knowing all attention is on us. The way I behave now will reflect not only on how they treat me but also on whether they allow Dean back into the fold. "Yes, sir."

"You've certainly grown up, my boy," Carlo tells Dean, still beaming. "You were quite different the last time we met."

"It's been a long time," Dean says.

His father looks to the floor, the smile gone. "That it has, my boy."

Dean catches my eye, likely trying to gauge my comfort level so far. But today isn't about me. It's about Dean. I'm here for support. Whether we kissed or not, I care about him. Friends care about each other, right?

"Well, come say hi to everyone." Carlo places his hand on Dean's back and leads us to the door. "Your cousin Rosa and the girls have prepared what I'm sure is a delicious meal."

Carlo walks us around to everyone, mostly to reintroduce Dean, although he adds, "This is Ethan," with no indication of our relationship. The rest of the group's reception to Dean is starkly different from Carlo's. Everyone is polite, but short.

"It's been awhile, Dino. Hope you've been well," a portly woman with dark hair and bright red lipstick says curtly.

"Happy Thanksgiving. Are you hungry?" a woman in an apron asks from behind the kitchen counter. She wipes her hands in the apron, her maroon-painted fingernails standing out against the white fabric. Rosa, I'm assuming, from the way she runs the kitchen.

The man sitting at the breakfast bar in a full suit with a drink in his hand simply nods to Dean and notes, "You've certainly grown up."

Nobody asks how he's been, where he's living, or what he's been up to in the nine years since he last spoke with them. And me? Nobody really addresses me beyond a smile or a simple, "Happy Thanksgiving." It makes me wonder what they think I'm doing here. *Did* Dean say we were together?

Carlo seems oblivious to it all, parading us around the room until Rosa yells from the kitchen that she's about to bring out the turkey.

"Everyone better sit!" she bellows. "I'm not dropping this thing when I carry it out!"

I stick close to Dean's side as we find seats. Besides Carlo, who insists Dean sit to his left, nobody seems too keen on sitting next to us. Everyone shuffles at the other end of the table, looking at one another as if completely stumped why there are just enough chairs for everyone. Nobody wants to verbalize why they're stalling, but it's still obvious.

The confusion ends when Frank Rizzoli—who is typing frantically on his phone—takes the seat to Carlo's right.

"Frankie, put that away," Carlo berates him. "Business can wait. We're about to enjoy a meal."

The seat to my left is empty until James fills it. Apparently he's the only one brave enough to sit by me. Then again, there isn't another option since Leon Wallace took the place across from me, right next to Rizzoli. They murmur quietly to each other but quickly stop when Carlo shoots them a warning look. I notice Joe Gotti, a large man with thick salt-and-pepper hair, sitting across the table to my left, talking to someone on the other end of the table. His arm is draped on the back of a chair in which a brunette woman is seated, so I assume she's his wife.

"Here it comes, watch yourselves!" Rosa calls as she and the other woman who was working in the kitchen with her carry out plate after plate of the feast. Several people comment on each plate.

"Oooh, looks delicious!"

"Green bean casserole, my favorite!"

"Who made this? You'll have to give me the recipe."

Once it's all set, Rosa takes a seat at the other end of the table and calls across to everyone, telling them to take more food.

"Rich, have another spoonful, I know you like those sweet potatoes. Mary Anne, what are you waiting for? Stuffing? Who's got the stuffing!"

Even after we've all filled our plates, the food doesn't seem to stop coming. The long table is soon filled with two large turkeys, bowls of vegetables, bread, pasta, and other sides.

I suppose part of the reason I eat so much is because I'm not participating in any of the conversation, which seems to be concentrated at the opposite end of the table. From what I've gathered, they're Dean's cousins. The women gush about their kids, the men talk about the work they've done to their houses, and eventually the whole group of them is cackling from reminiscing.

It strikes me how normal all of this seems. Besides the awkward vibe Dean and I bring to the table, this could be a Thanksgiving at anyone's house. It doesn't feel like a crime family's home. Then again, evidence of that might reveal itself later.

For instance, Frank Rizzoli could very well have been the one to invite a murderer into Dean's apartment. He might even be the murderer himself. The motive is the question, though. I wonder if it has anything to do with why Dean and I were invited to Thanksgiving dinner.

With the way everyone faces each other at Rosa's end of the table and the rest of us on Carlo's end all stare at our plates, it's clear that they're all just biting their tongues because that's what the boss wants them to do.

"The holidays get smaller each year," James mutters to me, breaking into my thoughts. "We used to fill this room up, but everyone started doing their own holidays as the family grew. Everyone here pretty much lives in the mall."

"The mall?"

He smiles. "Our little corner of the world here. It's a wonder the street isn't called Martelli Circle."

"Oh," I say with a smile. I try to think of something else to say, but James turns and starts up a conversation with someone on the other side of him.

"You want more, sweetie?" Rosa asks me, holding up a bread basket.

I tap my fork against the plate. "I'm still working at mine, thank you."

Glancing over at Dean's plate, I see that he's still picking away at his food too. He's silent and has that same tense look he did when we first walked in. I hesitate but finally tap the top of his thigh under the table.

He looks over at me and gives me a tight smile, but returns to his plate and keeps eating.

After a while, James passes me the pie Rosa has brought out and adds, "Rizzo says you're joining his team at Tranidek."

I nod, taking a piece of pumpkin from him. "Yeah, I start on Monday." Finally, something to talk about.

"That's a great company to work for." He rubs his thumb against the tips of his fingers. "Money, man."

I give a polite chuckle. "Well, I have bills, man." Stabbing into my pie, I ask, "What do you do?"

"Oh, I guess you could say I'm a serial entrepreneur. I find a need and start a business to fulfill that need. I actually just sold a company that makes a rubber wing, basically, that quiets the noise of windmills."

"Interesting. I didn't know that was a thing."

"Most people didn't!" he says with a laugh. "But I also own a few restaurants in the city, just to keep the cash flowing."

"Wow."

"Why don't you tell him the big news?" Gotti asks from across the table.

"What big news?" I ask, looking between the two. Gotti's eyes immediately go back to his plate.

"Well, it's not official yet, but I've decided to run for the open city council spot in the special election."

My eyes grow wide. "Oh. That's, uh, impressive. Good luck."

I wonder how many other competitors Myra will have to run against. Even though she said the council had some people in mind, I've been assuming that she was a shoo-in for the position. Now I'm not so sure.

"I know Myra Connors is in there now. She was great as Frank Lloyd's assistant, but I hardly think being the assistant is the same as actually being on the council."

"Really? I think she's doing a great job."

He flashes his yellow teeth in an almost condescending way. "It's been four days."

My cheeks flush and I look down at my plate. "Well, she comes from Hopman, which is the district she's representing, so I think she's perfect for the job."

"Oh, don't get me wrong. She's eager, but that will only go so far. She lacks the experience to take it to the next step and actually implement any sort of change."

Biting my tongue I say, "Well, we'll have to see how the election turns out." Arguing with him is not going to change his mind.

After dessert, when I'm sure the button on my pants won't hold up any longer, the girls begin clearing the dishes from the table, and half of the noise moves to the kitchen. Amid the commotion, Dean taps me on the shoulder as he stands, and I get up to follow him and his father out of the room.

Carlo leads us to the brick patio in the backyard, which is beautifully manicured. Mature oak trees create a sense of privacy, and what looks like a flower garden lines the edge of the fence at the back of the property. It makes me wonder what it looks like in the summer months, when everything is in bloom. The sun is setting, and the lights from the midtown buildings illuminate the sky.

We take our seats in cold metal chairs. The air is damp, but it doesn't seem to bother either of them, so I try to keep my chills out of my mind. Carlo pulls out a cigar from the inside of his jacket and offers each of us one, which we both decline.

"Suit yourself," he mutters between his lips as he lights his. He watches the city lights as he takes a couple puffs. "I want to apologize for the cold reception of my family this evening. I didn't give them much warning that you were coming. Clearly, some still have hard feelings."

"I understand," Dean replies. "But I assure you, you have nothing to worry about. With either of us. I've kept my promise thus far."

Carlo grins. "That you have, my boy."

"Father…" Dean starts, and the way he addresses his father—his *dad*—takes me by surprise. Was their relationship always this formal? Maybe that's why Dean took to his mom more.

"…why did you invite me today, after all these years?"

Carlo puffs on his cigar for a moment before responding. "I would like to ask you a favor. I know I haven't always been… supportive of your lifestyle, but I hope that inviting you and your partner to dinner will help show you that I'm willing to move past our differences. It's what your mother would've wanted."

His *what*? I suck in my lips and raise my eyebrows as the anger burns in me. Is that how Dean introduced me, or is that just what Carlo assumes? How many people tonight think that we're together? That must be why we were getting dirty looks all night. It's embarrassing.

I look over at Dean to give him a look that lets him know I'm annoyed, but he seems to be wrestling his own battle. I take a few deep breaths and push the anger away. I've reminded myself all evening that tonight isn't about me. It's about Dean.

"I appreciate that, sir," he responds.

"To be honest, I'm very surprised that this young man was the one keeping you company," Carlo goes on. "Funny how life works, isn't it?"

"Yeah," Dean mutters. He stares at the brickwork by his feet.

He's holding it all back, I can tell. All the hatred, all the remorse, all the revenge he'd like to get on his father. Disowned for nine years, only to be returned for a *favor*. Dean's a stronger person than that.

"I know this evening doesn't fix everything," Carlo continues. "I haven't been a perfect father. But then, you haven't been a perfect son."

I lean my chin against my fist and look away, chewing at the inside of my cheek. Now I'm holding back my hatred for Carlo.

Chapter Seven

Who says something like that? What a jackass. I hope Dean tells him to take his favor and shove it up his ass, because that's exactly what he deserves.

"The favor?" Dean pushes.

Carlo takes a few more puffs of his cigar and then continues. "I'm sure you've read in the papers how Michael Bello has gone rogue and turned against the family?"

This grabs my attention.

Dean nods. "I have. And I'm sure he's no longer in Olympia. Either he fled or you took care of him."

"Oh, I have no doubt that he's being protected. Wouldn't want anything to happen to their witness, would they?" Carlo flicks ash from the end of his cigar and smiles. "You know I don't normally encourage retaliation like that. It makes the police believe we have motivation to harm him."

"But you do," I say, despite myself.

Dean glares at me and then turns back to his father.

"You're going to wait him out."

Carlo points at his son. "Precisely. Bello is not a patient man. He'll do something that'll show his hand. Since he's the police's witness, I'm not the only one keeping an eye on him."

"So what do you need from me?"

"This is a special circumstance. Bello's a rat. He's been overstepping his boundaries for years. Up until recently, my time has been focused on maintaining the Martelli name in this city. My grandfather made this business what it is. Times have changed and so have we. But now that we no longer have competitors in Olympia, Bello's insubordination can't be ignored."

"What do you mean, insubordination?" Dean asks.

"For years Bello's been dealing drugs. I've known about this. Each time I confronted him, he claimed it was the gangs in Hopman and that he'd take care of it." Carlo shrugs. "I didn't care about drugs. If my capos want to make money on the side and it doesn't interfere with our main business, that's their own prerogative.

"What brought him to my attention was the prostitution rings he encouraged gang leaders to organize. Worse, he used *my money* to purchase the girls." Carlo shakes his head. "Mr. Pierce, you know very well my stance on prostitution. I couldn't stand by and let him do that. My men and I were organizing a plan to stop him when we heard that his drug shipment had been busted. But Bello was still free.

"I had some of my best men sit in on his capo meeting after the bust. I believe he's trying to organize a coup. We wanted to know what his plan was so we could teach him a lesson before he got too arrogant. That's when Olympia's very own Batman came in."

"Fuse?" Dean asks. There's a quiver in his voice. He was there that night too. Unmasked. If Carlo's men were there and saw him, there's no doubt they'd recognized him.

"Whatever his name is. The mission was compromised, so my men left."

"And now Bello's been released on a plea deal," Dean adds.

Carlo nods. "My hands are tied. Police surveillance is worse than ever. In the time it'll take for my men at the courthouse to clear this up for us, Bello will have gained a foothold in *my* market."

"So you want me to do your work for you? Collect your dues?"

"Of course not. Whether you changed your name or not, you're still Martelli by blood. Bello might've given the police information on you as well."

"Then what do you want me to do?"

"You've been out of this business for a long time, so nobody knows who you are. At least, not the men I want you to seek out. You're personable. I'm counting on that. Talk to people in Bello's district. Find out who was working for him."

"That's it?" Dean asks.

Carlo nods once. "My men will take it from there. Your mother would be very upset with me if she knew I was pulling you back into this."

"What about Bello's plea deal?"

"My contacts downtown will keep quiet whatever information he's given as long as possible, but we need to move quickly.

The more we know, the faster we can stop them."

"What does Dean get out of this?" So much for my vow of silence.

"I'm sure my son has told you that he was once ingrained in this family," Carlo says after another puff of his cigar. "The information the police may have on him could put him in prison as well."

My heart races at the thought. Dean's a good person. He's been out of the family for years. Wasn't in it that long, either. How bad could he have been? How desperate is the court system to put away Martelli and his men? Would they lock up someone like Dean to send a message?

Whatever it takes, I have to protect him. He's not going to get his clean name dirty again. Not when Fuse can step in.

Carlo blows out smoke through his nose. "Remember *omertà*."

Dean nods. "Of course, yeah."

I look away and roll my eyes. His family can't even look at him, but they expect him to keep their secrets? I guess that was more Carlo's call, but still. Couldn't they at least pretend to care about someone they used to call their cousin, nephew, or son?

"Enough business." Carlo rests his leg against his opposite knee. "Tell me what you've been up to."

Dean shrugs. "Working, I guess."

"I see you've become a physical therapist. Good for you. Is it your own company?"

"Not really. There's a group of us who work in the same office."

"And the pay is good?"

Dean nods. "Yes, it gives me enough to get by."

Puffing again at his cigar, Carlo nods. "Good. Good. Your mother would be very proud."

"Yeah." He looks down and picks at his nails. "She's been gone more than ten years already."

"It's hard to believe. Things were a lot different back then."

"Mm-hmm."

"But you, my boy, you've done well for yourself."

A hint of a smile cracks in the corner of Dean's mouth. "Thanks."

The exchange brings a smile to my face. Dean is happy talking to Carlo. No matter what, he's still his father. It's still just surface talk, but it's enough to bring a change to Dean's mood.

"What about you? How are things going?"

Carlo chuckles. "I'm not the young man I used to be. This business does that to you." He seems to remember I'm here and adds, "But nothing will stop this old man."

"Well, if getting shot didn't stop you when I was ten, I'm not sure anything would."

His father studies the bricks beneath our feet. "That really was a long time ago. Almost happened again a few years ago. Lost a friend of mine because of it. Horrible."

There seems to be genuine empathy in his voice. Maybe Carlo isn't completely heartless. Clearly not, from the way he welcomed his son back. It's odd to me, though, since I've built him up to be such a villain in my head. Someone with no compassion whatsoever.

Of course, just because he has compassion doesn't mean he typically acts on it. If anything, that makes things worse.

Carlo pulls back his sleeve and glances at his watch. "Well, it's getting late, and I take it none of my other guests care to join us out here."

He stands and we move back inside. I'm glad because my fingers and toes have long been numb.

"I hope Rosa set aside a dish for you to take," Carlo says when we're back in the sunroom.

"No, it's okay. I brought my bike, so I couldn't carry anything anyway," Dean says, but his father has already gone into the kitchen.

"Nice chat?" James asks from behind us.

We both jump. We didn't see him sitting in the wicker chair in the corner when we came in. Dean takes a step back, as tense as he was when we first arrived.

"Didn't mean to startle you," James says, squeezing Dean's arm. "It's been awhile, Dino. What've you been up to?"

"W-working," he mutters in response, recoiling from James' touch.

I want to say something to diffuse the situation, but something tells me it won't help. We just need to leave.

"Oh yeah. You were going to become a doctor or something, right?"

"He's actually a physical therapist," I cut in and take hold of Dean's hand. All thoughts about blurring the lines of our friendship go out the window. Right now, I just want to piss off James, for no other reason than the fact that he's making Dean feel uncomfortable.

I look over at Dean and smile. "That's how we met."

A faint snarl curls on James' lip, but he quickly ignores my comment and returns to Dean. "Well, clearly you've learned something." He eyes Dean up and down. "You've never looked better."

Carlo emerges from the kitchen with a paper plate in his hands and I quickly drop Dean's hand.

"Here we are," he says, handing Dean the plate. "Looks like everyone else took most of the leftovers. I had to dish you out some of mine."

"Thanks," Dean mutters.

"Thank you for having us." I lead us to the door and open it for Dean, letting him escape the situation as quickly as he can.

"Of course, Mr. Pierce," Carlo says. "Now that you're working for Frank, you're a friend of the family's."

Internally, I cringe. "I didn't see him leave."

"Rizzo? He had to take care of something for me." Carlo looks to the ground as he says it.

Got it. Rizzoli didn't like it that Dean was coming. I wonder what his attitude will be at work on Monday. Does he know that Dean and I are together—or rather that the family thinks we're together? We're definitely not together…

"Come on, Ethan, it's getting late," Dean urges.

"We can walk you out," James suggests.

We all pile out the door and stop dead. Perched like a rider racing through traffic, a skinned corpse sits on Dean's bike.

Chapter Eight

My jaw drops as all four of us stop in our tracks at the sight. Blood drips from the body down the side of Dean's bike. Luckily, the cold keeps the stench at bay, though the occasional wind gust still carries it our way.

Carlo's expression changes from shock to business in an instant. "Get it out of here," he tells James. "Get Gerald, Donny, whoever. Just get rid of it."

"Yes, sir." James jogs off toward one of the other houses in the circle.

"Should we call the police?" I ask, and then a second later realize my mistake.

Carlo glares at me and then looks at Dean. He turns away and rubs his forehead.

"I just thought it'd be better not to bring anymore suspi—" I stop midsentence when I see Dean shaking his head.

"Let's get inside," Carlo says, ushering us back into the house. "The boys will take care of this."

He leads us through a door off the dining room and takes the seat behind the large desk in the center of the room. It sits just in front of the large fireplace nestled between two windows overlooking the street. He motions to two plush leather chairs opposite the desk, and Dean and I each sit.

Carlo opens a drawer and pulls out a metal lockbox. Pulling out a wad of bills, he fans through it and hands it toward Dean. "Ride your bike home tonight and get it cleaned up tomorrow. Take it to Richard's on Elm. He won't ask questions."

"I'll be fine," Dean says. "You don't need to give me money."

"Just take it. Don't insult me." Carlo sets the bills in front of Dean.

Seeing the reluctance on Dean's face, I watch as he takes the money, folds it, and places it in his inside jacket pocket.

"Now, we won't have to worry about any witnesses. It's late, so only our neighbors might have seen—and we don't have to worry about them."

I watch as Carlo weighs his options, talking to no one in particular. This is how he and his family have taken over the city. Covering their tracks, strong-arming people into doing their bidding and letting the family's illegal practices slip by unnoticed.

"It's dark, but there are streetlights. If someone saw the body carried in—"

"Who do you think it was?" Dean asks.

Carlo seems to just remember we're sitting here. "Oh, I'm not sure." He leans back and pulls at the curtains on the window. "Looks like the boys have removed it. Let me get you some towels to clean up."

Dean doesn't meet my eyes when he stands and follows his father out to the garage. Carlo pulls a couple rags from a drawer at the work bench and hands them to Dean.

"Don't fuss with it too much. You just don't want blood on your clothes. Is your parking secure?"

Dean nods. Since Cale knows he's been staying with us—and since neither of us drive—we've been letting Dean use our one designated parking spot beneath our building. It's dark and uncrowded. Perfect for a vehicle that might still have blood on it.

"Good. Wipe the seat and get home. Take it to Richard's

tomorrow as soon as you can. If you have to, tell him it's a favor for me, but only if you have to."

Dean nods, and we walk through the open garage door to his bike.

I help him wipe up the blood as best we can. The smell is still present but not unbearable. I try to get a sense of what's going through Dean's mind, but I can't tell. Scared is my guess, just like I am.

The first time I get a moment alone with him is when we return to the kitchen in Carlo's house to wash our hands clean.

"How're you doing?" I mutter to him under the noise of the faucet.

"Fine."

"Dean—"

"We'll talk at home," he snaps.

Outside, Carlo kisses each side of Dean's face again and pulls him in for another hug. After parting, he shakes my hand and tells me, "Take care of him."

It's all an illusion, because Dean and I aren't together. We're friends. Carlo's words imply there's more. But I ignore all of that and simply say, "I will."

Dean's already mounted his bike and revved it up by the time I part from his father. Apparently staying here is a worse thought for him than riding a bike that just held a bloody corpse.

My arms are barely around his waist before he flies out of the driveway and down the street.

———

THE APARTMENT IS dark when we get home, which I'm grateful for. I need to talk to Dean, and Cale would've been an excuse not to. Was tonight a typical evening at the Martelli household? No wonder Dean wanted to escape.

We're silent as we get ready for bed. It's late, but I know we have to talk tonight. If we wait until morning, the impact of facing Dean's family and finding the body will have worn off. I know my hands are still shaking from seeing it. I can't imagine how I'm going to sleep tonight. Talking to Dean will be the perfect distraction, and I have to do it before I lose my edge to ask for the answers I really want.

Dean fans out the sheet on the couch as he prepares his bed. I clear my throat to get his attention. "Tonight was interesting."

He tosses a pillow at one end. "Yeah."

"What are your thoughts on your father asking for help?"

He shrugs. "I don't know. I'll have to think about it."

"Right, yeah."

Taking a seat on the edge of the couch, he pulls out his phone and scrolls through. I can't tell if he's trying to give me a sign that he's not interested in a conversation. With my heart pounding and my ears burning, I step toward him and take a seat on the edge of the couch. "Part of the reason you left the family business is because you're gay, isn't it?"

This snaps his attention back to me. "Why do you say that?"

Fighting to maintain my courage, I say, "Clearly, everyone thought I was your boyfriend."

He tosses his phone on the cushion to his right and comes to sit on the arm of the couch next to me. I don't move.

"Sorry about that," he says. "Are you mad?"

"I definitely felt the tension," I admit. "Add that to all the mafia stuff, and it's no wonder you left."

"Yeah."

"How'd it feel? Being back?"

"Definitely weird. I grew up in that house. That was my mom's kitchen. It's been a long time. To see my cousins working in it…" He shrugs.

"Do you miss them?"

"Who? The family who barely looked me in the eyes? No."

"Not even your father? I saw you tonight. You loved it that you guys were talking again. At dinner you were stiff, but when it was just the three of us, you were yourself."

He sighs. "Seeing him again tonight was nice. But it's not real. The holidays are about the only time he sets aside the business—at least in front of the family. So no, I wasn't myself. Not really. Just a projection of the person he wanted to see."

I look down, my voice tiny. "Because he didn't ask about me?"

He doesn't answer me. Instead, he studies his hands, picking at the corners of his nails. "I never thanked you for coming tonight," he finally says. "I really appreciate it."

"Of course."

"I knew it probably wasn't the way you wanted to spend your Thanksgiving, but I needed you there."

Where would I be if I wasn't with Dean tonight? At my parents' house, fending off questions about how I'm holding up after Emma, how my recovery from the lightning strike is doing, and how I got fired. Instead, I got to spend the evening without any of that. For the first time since I met him, Dean was the center of attention.

My mind replays the way Dean acted tonight. Closed off from everyone except his father.

"Do you mind if I ask you something?" I start, trying to build up the courage to broach what I know will likely be an uncomfortable topic for him. But after what we just endured, all of this is uncomfortable territory.

"Sure," he mutters.

"What's the deal between you and that James guy? The real story." I glance up at him and see that same terrified expression on his face. The one that strikes me to my core every time I see it.

"Why do you ask?"

"Well, he said he's going to run for city council. I thought you might know something I should pass along to Myra. If he's working with your father, I can't imagine he plays fair."

Dean shakes his head. "No. I don't have anything."

I narrow my eyes. "Are you sure? You're weird about him. There's a reason you're afraid of him—"

"I'm not afraid of him."

"Dean, you didn't think he'd be there tonight. I could tell as soon as he answered the door. That look on your face…I hated it." I turn up my hands. "You don't have to tell me, but you can't deny that something about him triggers you."

Chapter Eight

I start to get up, but Dean catches my arm and pulls me to him.

Close.

Too close. Like we're going to—

His lips are on mine, kissing me with more vigor than the previous two kisses we've shared. Resisting the urge to push him away, I give in to it. My arms wrap around him and I pull him toward me. It's different tonight. We've grown closer. And we've been here before. I'm still scared, but not as much as I was the last time we kissed.

He stands and we shuffle backward, our lips locked firmly together, as we move to my bedroom. We break long enough to readjust on the bed and then *I'm* the one pulling him back for more.

Rational thinking has escaped me, and I let myself give in to him. Everything that's kept me up at night for the last week is out of my mind. In this moment, it's just me and him.

He works my shirt off and I don't stop him. My hands wander across his body, pulling him closer, never feeling like he's close enough. Never feeling like I've had enough.

"You okay?" he asks with ragged breaths, his hands running along my thighs.

I nod. "Yeah. Keep going."

Chapter Nine

Why am I like this? Why did I just spend the night with Dean? Worse, why did I like it?

I've been lying here for at least an hour, trying to figure out how exactly I got to this moment. How did I go from being perfectly content with Emma a couple weeks ago to sleeping with someone I didn't even *know* a couple months ago?

I'm just lonely, that's all it is. Even though Emma's only been gone a week and a half, I've spent more than a month without her. Wondering whether or not she'd even survive. Mourning her when she didn't. Yesterday was my first holiday without her. I needed something to distract myself.

Never mind the fact that the whole time I was at dinner, I never once thought of her. I spent yesterday among people who routinely associate with the man behind Emma's murder. Hell, with as much as they double-cross one another, I could've been dining with someone who played a part in her death.

No, I can't blame Dean. That's not fair. He didn't murder her. I know that, despite what I accused him of before. He's too good of a person for that. That's part of the reason we're friends.

Chapter Nine

Friends.

Nothing more. Just friends.

The sudden realization that I'm lying naked in bed with my supposed *friend* makes me get to my feet. It's five in the morning, but I don't care. I can't lie here and act like this is normal anymore.

If I can sneak out, maybe I can pretend it never happened. Life can go back to the way it was.

As I pull on my clothes, Dean stirs.

"Where are you going?" he grumbles, his eyes only slits.

I lick my cracked lips. "Just running to the bathroom. Go back to sleep."

He tucks the blanket over his shoulder and rolls over. With one last look in his direction, I slip out the door.

The late November air hits me hard when I step outside. A part of me feels like I deserve to be uncomfortable after what I just did, but being mopey isn't going to help anyone—least of all, Emma. Nothing can help her anymore.

The bus ride out to Terry Lake is shorter than I anticipated. Probably because there's no one on the road this early in the morning. After I reach my stop, it's another ten-minute walk to Emma's gravesite. The grass hasn't had a chance to grow over it yet, so the unearthed dirt is coated with snow.

There's a flower pot filled with frost-bitten flowers. Her family must've brought them yesterday. I should've come yesterday too.

I shake my head, trying to stop myself from having these regrets. I can't change the past. Only the future. I'm here now. I'll just have to make sure to visit her more frequently from now on. I owe it to her. To her memory.

I sit by Emma's grave for an hour before I get up and head back into the city. I've daydreamed about the past long enough. There's work to do. There are now two bodies to investigate.

Not wanting to go home and risk seeing Dean, I head toward the clinic. I picked up a newspaper before boarding my bus back into the city and saw that the identity of the first body was released this morning. Lee Howes.

Fuse: Omertà

The name doesn't ring any bells, so once I get into my basement hideout at the clinic, I hack into the Grid to dig up more dirt on him. The Grid is where the city backs up all of its documents on every resident. There are loads of firewalls to get through, so it always takes me some time to hack into it.

There was no one here when I got in, but it isn't long before I hear Alex's familiar heels clicking upstairs. I'm not positive where things stand with me and her, but if I had to choose between her and Dean, she's the one I'm willing to face right now.

But only when she approaches me first. Right now, I have work to do.

The information I pull up on Howes shows that he's thirty-five and lived just north of downtown in the oldest residential district in the city. The area is famous for its brick townhouses and narrow cobblestone streets. After a period of disrepair and decay, the neighborhood was revitalized in the seventies piece by piece. Today it's an affluent community, and some of the richest residents in the city live there.

Okay, so the guy had money. I guess that could be a reason for someone to kill him. But why the public display? Is the murderer just a sociopath? Could be, but I'm willing to bet there's more to it than that.

I dig deeper, hacking into his bank accounts, and find direct deposits from the First Olympian National Bank. Right where his body was found.

Maybe Howes' death was a giant middle finger to the bank? According to the bank's website, Howes was a loan officer. Could be that the murderer was denied a loan and wanted to get revenge. But then, why wouldn't he just rob the bank? Why kill Howes? There must've been another reason, but it may very well be that I can't find the answer online.

I lean back with my hands on the back of my head and stare at the computer. I wish I had taken a better look at Dean's apartment when we first discovered someone was squatting. There were likely clues there that I could use now to identify who the murderer is.

I reach for my phone and consider texting Dean, but I set

it back down instead. There are other connections to the murderer that we know—or rather, suspect. Like, for instance, that he could have ties with Frank Rizzoli. But that could also just be a coincidence.

Still, the clues pointing to him are too perfect to pass up. The murderer is using Dean's apartment and Rizzoli has money tied to that building. The second body was found right outside Martelli's house. Rizzoli was there that night and left because he had to take care of something for Carlo.

Tapping the side of my phone, I follow that train of thought to Michael Bello. What if he's the one killing people? Or rather, someone working for him. Dropping a body under Martelli's nose certainly sends a message. If Bello really is planning a coup, he'd need to have an in with someone in the family. Rizzoli could be that in.

But I'm not convinced. Frank Rizzoli has presumably been loyal to Carlo for a long time. How else would he achieve such a high ranking position in the family? What would make him want to turn his back on arguably the most powerful man in Olympia?

Frustrated, I decide to continue with my search on Howes. His Facebook profile is simple to hack into. "Password123" is not the most secure. You'd think someone who works at a bank would know that, but that might just be the IT tech in me talking.

His profile says he's single, but otherwise there isn't much. Awkward selfies, clearly only taken for a Facebook profile picture. A couple before and after gym pictures. Several photos of his cat. A few of his photos have filters for different causes. A pink ribbon, a rainbow, the French flag. He mostly likes and shares memes and comments on various news posts—nothing that really paints a solid picture of him, though. Nothing to indicate why someone would want to murder him. The best I could find was that Howes was outraged when the city invested millions into the solar roadway project. But then, before it was implemented and proven to be a success, a lot of people were against it. Was he just the unfortunate one who got jumped? But if that's the cause, why wait until now?

I scroll through the few messages he has. Only a handful. From a woman—presumably his sister, based off of the shared last name—asking if he was coming to Thanksgiving, dated the day before his death. A few older ones making arrangements to meet up. Again, nothing that strikes me as reason for someone to kill him. Quickly scrolling through his friends list does me no good either.

The password for his email account isn't as easy as the one for his Facebook account. I'm about to try my hacker tricks to get into it when I hear the door at the top of the stairs swing open.

In a flurry, I close out of all my tabs and turn around.

"Jumpy?" Alex asks as she crosses the room, coffee in hand.

I let out a breath of air. "I've got a lot on my mind."

"About the body you found the other day?" She sees my expression and adds, "Wes told me you saw it."

"Yeah. The police released the name of the victim, but I couldn't find much online about him."

"Something will come up," she says, taking a seat next to me. "Or maybe the police will figure it out first and take care of it."

She's trying to be more open to me being Fuse. I know that. But her comment about the police reveals that she's still hoping I'll give all this up.

The fact of the matter is, I *need* to wear the suit. Especially after meeting Dean's family and finding the second corpse, I can feel the twinges of electricity flowing through my body. The suit will help regulate the charges. And if I'm putting it on, I might as well do some good with it too.

"What brings you in here so early?" She leans back and sips her coffee.

I shrug. "Lots of stuff."

"Emma?"

"Yeah." I keep my eyes on my fingers fidgeting in my lap.

"It'll get easier."

"I know." The conversation is getting dangerously close to

what's really bothering me, so I ask her, "What did you do for Thanksgiving?"

"Went to my parents' house in Jurek. My sister and her husband were there with their kids, so I got to see my nieces."

"That's good. And then you're back here bright and early today. Always working."

"I'm a doctor. I can't turn it off. Besides, like you're one to talk."

"What?" I smirk.

"What are you doing here so early?"

"The body. I told you that." I try to feign a laugh but it falls flat.

She leans forward to catch my attention. "What's really going on, Ethan? Did you not have a good day yesterday?"

"It was fine," I say quickly.

"Did you go see your parents or did you stay home with Cale?"

I clear my throat and consider lying to her. The truth will come out eventually, and if Alex is ever going to be okay with Dean, I shouldn't lie about him. That would tell her there's something about him I want to keep hidden.

"Um, actually, I went to Dean's."

"Dean?" Her voice rises. "His apartment?"

"No," I mutter, my mind flashing to the mess we discovered at his place. Besides that, I'm nervous and I'm not sure why. I'm an adult. I can make my own choices. "To his…um…father's house."

Rising to her feet, she places her free hand on her hip and bellows, "You went to the mob boss's house for Thanksgiving dinner? What the hell is the matter with you?"

"Dean's father called him and invited him. They haven't spoken since Dean was a teenager."

"And you believe him?"

"I don't have any reason not to."

"He *lied* to you, Ethan!" she yells. "He *knew* you were investigating his family and he kept his mouth shut. Now, all of a sudden, after—what, one talk?—everything is smoothed over? No, I don't believe it."

"Believe it, because it's true," I say, my own voice rising now. "The way everyone reacted to him at dinner yesterday means Dean's story checks out."

"And what about you? What if you get seen out and about with him and word gets out that Dean's a Martelli? The police already know. If he gets caught with something and you're with him—"

"Dean hasn't done anything for the family business in a long time."

"Then why did his father ask him to dinner after so long?" she counters. "If they really haven't spoken, he's not just going to invite Dean to dinner without looking for something in return."

"You don't understand," I mutter.

"You're right. I don't understand why you're still talking to him. You said he's an asset to you, but I think you're not seeing things clearly. He's going to get you in trouble, and I'd hate to see that happen."

Refusing to meet her eyes, I stare at the floor. I try to picture life without Dean. I can't. And listening to Alex criticize him lights a fire in me. Beckons me to stand up for him. I would've done the same for Emma.

But why am I comparing them?

"Help me understand," Alex says in a softer voice. She sits on the chair and moves in closer to me. "Ethan, I realize it seems like I'm always yelling at you, but it's only because I care about you. I don't want to see you get hurt. To me, it looks like Dean is just a dark path for you."

I shake my head, chancing a look up at her. "He's not, though. I trust him."

She bites her bottom lip. "Please don't be mad when I ask this, but"—she sighs—"are you and Dean...*together*?"

"No," I say as a reflex. My heart pounds, and I back up and rise to my feet. "I'm not fucking gay. You don't know what you're talking about."

Before I realize what I'm doing, my feet are carrying me to the staircase. I need to get out of here.

Chapter Nine

"Ethan," she moves toward me, but I race up the stairs. "I'm sorry! Please come back!"

It's too late. I'm already outside. The wind is freezing, but I don't notice. I'm boiling with rage. Embarrassment.

Is it obvious? Am I wearing a sign on my forehead that broadcasts that Dean and I have kissed? That we've slept together? Do people talk about us behind our backs? Has their perception of me changed because of it? Should I even care? I've got enough other things to worry about.

But I do care. Cale, Myra, Alex—everyone in my life. If they knew what Dean and I have done, would they be okay with it? Would I be okay if they weren't? Is Dean worth risking other relationships in my life for? Haven't I lost enough? And what about Emma? Did I disrespect her memory by being with someone else?

It doesn't matter. Dean and I are not dating. Last night was a one-time deal. A moment of weakness. It's never happening again.

CHAPTER TEN

I peer around the corner of a long-empty building down Adams Street. Two rowdy crowds face each other in the dark. One standing in the middle of the street, the other in front of a dilapidated house.

I strain to listen to the conversation, but I'm too far to hear anything. Instead, I watch and wait for something to happen. And something *will* happen. They're not exactly selling Girl Scout cookies.

One of the guys by the house brandishes a gun, which is my cue. Running around the back of the building, I jump over a fence in the side parking lot and end up in a vacant, overgrown lot. The two gangs are only two lots down from me. Crouching down, I try to stick to the shadows as I move closer.

"Fuck Bello," I hear one of them say. "This is *our* street now."

Jumping over another fence, I land in the backyard of the dilapidated house. One of the guys on the street must've heard me and takes notice. Everyone moves. Some scramble to a car parked on the street, others dash inside the house, and two of them chase after me.

Chapter Ten

Someone emerges from the back door, which isn't far from me.

"Who the hell are you?" he yells.

Sprinting around the side of the house, I stop short when I see one of the guys from the street pointing his gun at me. He fires just as I dive to the ground, and the bullet whizzes over my head. I shoot a quick jolt of lightning his way and he falls to the ground, convulsing.

More shots fire from the windows of the house, and I press against the wall to cover myself. Most of the guys from the street are gone, though I notice a few of them ducking behind cars for cover.

I'm stuck. I have to somehow get the upper hand, but they outnumber me by a long shot. I thought I'd be able to pick them off one by one from a secure location, but obviously that plan is out the window. Maybe if I—

Another gunshot. The bullet hits the house less than a foot away from where I stand.

Dropping to the ground, I move to the back of the house and zap the guy standing on the back steps. Pushing him aside, I race inside.

The slanted floors throw me off at first, but I manage to tuck inside a laundry closet before anyone spots me.

"Hey, Mick, you see anything?"

There's no answer. Mick must be the one on the back steps. I wonder just how many guys are inside.

When the voice steps into the room, I drive my fist into his face and use the cord from the iron to restrain him. Pressing my finger to my ear, I call 9-1-1 through my com and immediately hang up.

A punch in my back just below my shoulder blade tells me I made too much noise restraining the first guy. I spin around and face the two men in the small room. I send a quick jolt of lighting into each one's gut and they fall like rocks.

Stepping into the next room, I hear the click of a gun just before it's pressed against my head. My heart pounds in my chest.

"Real slow, Halloween. Real slow," the man behind the gun says.

"Okay, okay." I hold my hands up, and the gun shifts as he flinches.

"Easy with those hands! You kill my boys?"

I shake my head slightly. "No. They'll be fine."

"They better be."

"What's with the powwow outside?"

"Ross Street fuckers think they can move into our turf."

"Now that Bello's gone?"

He's quiet for a moment and then, "All right, you know some stuff. Doesn't matter, though, cause I'm about to blow your fucking head off."

Police sirens grow louder, which draws his attention out the window. Knocking the gun from his hand, I grab his arm, pulling it back behind him, and slam his face against the wall.

"What were you going to do?" I ask.

He snarls, and I hit him with a jolt of electricity. I can feel my body weaken, but that's okay. The cops are here so my job is done. Still, I pull off his belt and restrain his hands behind his back.

Blue lights flash through the front window, and I race out the back and vault over the fence. I climb to the top of an apartment building three blocks over to catch my breath and take in the area. The blue lights from Adams Street stand out, and I breathe a sigh of relief that I *didn't* get my head blown off.

Gang violence has been increasing in Hopman since Bello was arrested. Luckily, the facial recognition software has been helping me identify the biggest gang leaders in the neighborhood. The Ross Street and Adams Street gangs were only two of many in the neighborhood. I doubt they'll all be arrested, but hopefully my presence will scare some of them.

Looking out away from the Hopman neighborhood, I notice one of the spotlights on the upper tier of city hall flashing. I watch it to make sure, and it flashes again.

Glancing down at the street below, everything seems quiet—besides Adams Street—but I don't know if anything else will happen tonight. Hopefully news of Fuse being out and about has scared off anyone else thinking of causing ruckus. If not, the police lights will do the trick.

Chancing it, I climb down the back fire escape and run to city hall, doing my best to stick to the shadows. Still, I know a few people catch a glimpse of me as I get farther into the core of the city. Mostly I hear, "That's him!" or "He *is* real!"

There's no fire escape up city hall, but I manage to find the side staircase I used when I visited Myra as Fuse. I thought I had figured out which floor the flashing light was coming from, but when I step out of the staircase inside, the floor is dark and quiet. Still, I recognize it as Myra's so I decide to investigate.

The main office space is empty. There's only one private office with a light on, but that's empty too. When I step back out to the main area, Myra is crawling from a window that overlooks the ledge where one of the spotlights sits. It's kind of a funny sight since she's still dressed in a black skirt and white blouse.

She pulls down the window and sighs as she looks out. I don't know the best way to get her attention without scaring her, but she's seen Fuse before.

"Looking for someone?" I lean against the doorway of the private office with my arms crossed.

She lets out a yelp and holds her hand to her chest. After a few deep breaths she says, "You, actually."

"We're going to have to come up with a better system, then."

"I'm not planning on making this a regular thing." She keeps her distance, but she seems calm. "I just wanted to thank you for whatever part you played in putting Frank Lloyd and Michael Bello behind bars."

"What do you care about Michael Bello?"

"He had a tight grip on the district I oversee, which was detrimental to improvement. Now that he's gone, I can really get to work on making life better for those residents. For that, I want to say thank you."

It feels good to get some recognition as Fuse. Exactly when I needed it, too.

"You're welcome, but Michael Bello is free now."

"Even so," she says, "a conviction takes a toll on a person's reputation."

"Hopefully that'll do it." I move to leave, but she speaks up.

"I feel like a thank you isn't enough, though."

"It's more than I was expecting. I don't do this for gratitude."

"Then why do you do this?" She plays with the ring on her right hand. "I know you haven't been doing it for long, but you're starting to become a symbol of hope for people. I want to be a part of that. I want to help you."

I shake my head, almost say her name. "No. Your job is here in this office. Mine is out there." I point out the window.

"But I've helped before—even if I didn't know I was at the time. Let me help again."

I need to put a stop to this. I can't let Myra get involved anymore. Especially now that she's an acting council member. She's got her sights set on bigger goals. I won't be the one who brings it all crashing down. Not with James Alexander about to announce his run for council. She needs to focus on her election.

Of course, it might help her campaign if she uncovers something big, like she did with Frank Lloyd and Michael Bello. The high from that is subsiding. She needs something else.

But as much as it'd be a huge help, she can't look into the bodies. I still haven't determined who is behind them and until I know who the enemy is, I can't risk Myra's safety. There is, however, something else she could do for me. For Dean.

"Michael Bello."

"Of course," she says eagerly. "What about him?"

"I need to know which drug dealers and gang leaders were working for him before he was arrested. But all I'm asking you to do is gain intel. Don't go out looking for these people. Everything I'm asking you to do, you can do right here in this office."

She nods. "Of course, yeah."

I study her a moment, debating whether I should warn her about Alexander's intent to run for council, but that might connect me as Ethan with Alexander—especially if she found out who I spent Thanksgiving with. Instead, I head toward the door and tell her, "Be careful."

Chapter Ten

"What are you going to do with the information once I get it?" she asks to my back.

I turn. "Don't worry about it."

———

IT'S ALMOST ONE in the morning by time I head home. Besides handling some of the theater crowd who allowed alcohol to transform them from law-abiding citizens to thugs, I was also keeping an eye out in case another body showed up. I still haven't found a connection between the two—not that I know the name of the second one—and now that I've had time to dwell on it, where we found the last body makes me more than a little nervous.

The first body just happened to be found right across the street from where Dean and I were standing watch. Outside the office Cale was in. The second body was sitting right on Dean's bike, while we were both inside.

Of course, the first body was placed where crowds of people travel every day. There's no telling who the bodies were meant to be seen by. Maybe Dean. Maybe me. But if the bodies were meant for me, that means whoever placed them knows I'm Fuse and is watching me. How else would they know I was on the roof of the Stanley Hotel or at Martelli's house?

In an effort to further conceal my identity, I make sure to change out of my Fuse suit in Chester Park. It's dark and empty so late in the night, so it offers the perfect concealment. At least enough to take off the Fuse boots, gloves, and mask and cover the main part of the suit with my regular clothes. Short of the black material showing under my shirt, nobody knows what I'm wearing underneath.

As I walk down the hallway to my apartment, it hits me how exhausted I am. The whole floor is quiet, and the sound of my footsteps seems to echo throughout the building.

I wonder if Dean is asleep already. A part of me hopes he is, just to avoid the awkward conversation, but another part of me feels bad for avoiding him all day. I should talk to him soon. Set some boundaries or something.

As I reach for my keys in my pocket, I notice a large envelope taped to the front door. *Cale Pierce* is written on it. I turn it over and see that it's unsealed.

Inside is a picture of a half-rotten hand. Almost leathery, the skin is an ugly black and oozes with what I can only assume is pus. Dried blood is caked along the few lacerations and especially where it should be connected to an arm.

On the reverse side of the photo is a typed letter.

Dear Sir,

We know that you've been asking questions about certain developments in north Olympia. If it is your wish to continue, it is our promise that you'll have to be silenced.

Yours,
Black Hand

Black Hand? Is that Leon Wallace? Or maybe someone else on his team? What exactly went on in that meeting? Dean and I watched it, but we had no way of knowing what they discussed. We should've bugged it somehow.

I have to show this to Cale. No matter what, he needs to know that they don't like his questions. He has to know he's being threatened. I just lost Emma, I can't lose him too.

Chapter Eleven

ey, Dean, wake up." He's wrapped in the blanket on my bed, and he jumps when I wake him.

"What is it? What's going on?" He sits up and looks around, confused.

"I found this on the door." I hand him the envelope and take in how comfortable he is in my bed. As if he thinks we're together. Which he probably does. Running away from him all day didn't exactly tell him that it was a one-time deal.

He rubs his eyes before he pulls the letter out and reads it. I lean against my dresser and watch his reaction. His eyes grow wide, and he runs a callused hand through his short-cropped hair.

"Ethan, this is not good."

"I know. What's the significance of the hand?"

"*La Mona Nera*, or the Black Hand, was a way the mafia in New York used to threaten people into paying sums of money." He waves the picture. "Blackmail."

"Okay, but this Black Hand isn't asking for money. They want him to stop researching the Works. Do you think this is your father's doing?"

He scrunches his face and shakes his head. "I don't think so. I'm not sure he would threaten your brother right after he asked me for a favor. Not when he knows about us."

Us.

"Besides," he continues, "with Bello going rogue, this might actually be his doing."

My heart rate quickens and I worry that he's targeting Cale because he knows I'm Fuse. But it still doesn't make sense.

"How do you figure?"

"Well, he's probably in witness protection, like my father said, so he could be hiding behind the Black Hand to keep his name out of it. He's probably still in touch with people who could've planted this."

"Okay, but why would he care whether Cale looks into the Works? I mean, his scandal has already been made public. Bello was a huge part of the underground casino your family used to run there. Unless he later used it as a crack house, I can't imagine there's much worse to be exposed. Sounds to me like this is Leon Wallace."

"Bello knows you're Fuse. Maybe this is his way of sending a message to you."

I look down at my feet because I don't want to confirm or deny what he's saying. Instead, I change directions. "Has anyone in your family ever written a Black Hand letter?"

Dean shakes his head. "Not really. My father likes to make things personal. He sends capos or soldiers to extort money from people in their districts."

"Oh, well at least he stays to chat before he robs them." I roll my eyes, but Dean's still staring at the letter.

"He offers them protection in exchange. Like an added tax."

"Still wrong."

"Never said it wasn't. But my father said people would be more willing to trust him if they knew him personally. Actually, a lot of people are glad to pay him. People know he has connections. If they have a problem of any kind, he'll find a way to help them. So long as they pay their dues."

"What does he protect them from?"

"He keeps the streets clear. Think about it. Olympia has problems, sure, but not nearly as bad as some cities. The bulk of our crime rate is focused in Hopman, which, as you know, Bello didn't keep in the best shape. He had side deals of his own."

It makes sense. Michael Bello was encouraging drug deals and prostitution through gangs, all while hiding under the decay of that part of the city.

"Didn't your father ever suspect Bello wasn't being honest about his efforts to get rid of the gangs?"

He shrugs. "Maybe. Probably. He's definitely suspicious now."

"Do you think he's chosen a new capo already?"

Dean chews on his thumbnail. "Maybe. I still need to figure out how to find the names of the gang leaders."

"Um, about that…"

His face flashes with anger. "What did you do?"

"Well, Myra called Fuse to city hall—"

"How did she call you to city hall?"

"Search light."

"Right," he says disbelievingly.

"Anyway, she said as a thank you for me helping expose Lloyd—and Bello—that she wanted to do something for me. So I suggested she look into the gang leaders Bello had been working with so you don't have to."

Dean rubs his face and lets out a frustrated breath of air. "Ethan, that was incredibly stupid. Why would you do that?"

"I thought Myra would be able to hide behind her position at city hall, and it would keep your name clear."

"The difference is, *I* can handle myself! I know what to expect with some of those men!"

"Really? Is that why you're hiding out in my apartment?"

"That's different."

"How?"

"Because I know what I'm up against! Getting Myra mixed into something this serious is just moving the target from me to her."

I look out the window. He has a point. I definitely considered it, but I thought since she wasn't leaving the office she'd be okay. I rationalized it so I'd feel better, but I could've just put Myra in serious danger.

He stands, clad only in his underwear, and steps toward me, hooking his arm around my waist.

"I appreciate you looking out for me, but let's just forget that for now." His tone is softer. "I want to talk about last night. Well, this morning, rather. I know why you ran off. It's going to take some adjusting, but—"

I step back and push at his hard chest. "No, Dean. This isn't—we're not together."

"Oh." He nods his head slightly. "Yeah, we should probably have that talk. If you just want to take it slow until we see where things go—"

"No," I repeat, forcing myself to meet his eyes. "This isn't ever going to be a thing."

He looks sad, but still doesn't look too surprised by my reaction. "Ethan, you're just scared. I'm not saying you have to be with me forever, but last night was proof that you're at least curious."

"I'm not!"

"That's not the impression I got when we were—"

"I wasn't—" I let out a breath of air. "Look, it was a one-time deal, that's it. It didn't mean anything. It was just sex."

The hurt look in his eyes spreads across his face. He takes a step back from me. "Oh."

I rub my forehead. That was too harsh. "Dean, I'm sor—"

"It's fine," he says quickly. "Yeah, totally cool." He gathers his clothes from the chair in the corner.

"It's just that with everything with Emma and being Fuse—"

"Don't worry about it." He flashes me a sad smile quickly before brushing past me to the living room. "I'll crash on the couch."

An awful feeling encapsulates me as I follow him out to the living room. "No, you don't have to. I'll sleep on the couch."

"I'm tired," he says, ignoring me. "I should get some sleep."

I linger as I watch him lie down out of my view. Whether

we're together or not, I hate seeing him upset. He's my friend. My best friend, really. I don't want him to be sad. Especially not because of me.

If nothing else, I can say I definitely put an end to the idea of there being an *us*. Maybe a little too well.

———

DEAN'S GONE BY the time I wake up late the next morning. I'm disappointed but not surprised. I was hoping to apologize for what I said and clarify where we stand. I still need his help. I still want to be friends with him. I'm just not attracted to him. At least, I don't want to be. I don't know. I wasn't exactly pretending the other night, but the whole thing just feels… strange.

What I need to do is go back to what I'm used to. Find a girl who'll get my mind off of Dean until the feelings just go away.

My workout schedule has completely gone off the rails since Emma died and everything got weird with Dean. Today is another day I go solo to the gym. It's Saturday, so I can take as long as I need. All of my angst is perfect fuel for my run. It feels like all the stress I'm under seeps out of my pores with my sweat. Getting my blood flowing and my heart pumping helps me clear my head, frees my mind to think over the next steps I can take in figuring out who's been dropping bodies around the city. I'm not a detective, so I'm sure there are obvious leads I haven't chased down yet. Still, since I'm Fuse I know more than the average person, like who exactly is involved with the Martellis and what some of their motives are.

Michael Bello is still a prime suspect, but a number of things still don't add up with that. Namely, how would he do it? If he's in witness protection, he's not even in this area anymore, but it might not be hard for him to call on his people now to do his bidding.

The other question I still can't answer is why the murderer is even doing this to begin with. Bello would certainly have reason if he's trying to send a message to the Martellis, but why would he make the attack so public when he's already provided information to the police?

The stitch in my side pulls me out of my head. I hit the red "Stop" button on the treadmill and catch my breath before taking a sip of water.

The Black Hand letter bothers me too. How long does Cale have to stop his research? Rather, how long do I have to convince him? And how will they know he's stopped? How closely are they watching him? Us?

I do some exercises with the dumbbells, but what I'd really love to do again is some kind of combat training. I'm doing okay on my trips out as Fuse, but I'm certainly no expert. Too bad I don't have my training partner.

Snow flurries float in the wind as I walk home. December is next week. Christmas decorations hang in the windows of some of the storefronts I pass.

It doesn't feel like the Christmas season should be here already. Emma's the reason, mostly. I miss her like crazy. I'd grown accustomed to her singing off-key to Christmas carols or bringing cutout cookies to the office during the holidays.

Cale's home by time I get out of the shower. He's hunched over his laptop at the kitchen counter, typing up what I can only imagine is his latest news report. He mutters a hello to me, but otherwise ignores me, too focused on getting his thoughts to paper.

Still no sign of Dean, though. I wonder if I'll see him tonight at all. A part of me hopes I do, but another part of me wants to put as much distance between us as possible.

Forcing myself to push forward, I snatch the envelope from the top of the dresser in my room and flick it against my open palm as I consider the best way to bring it up to Cale. There really isn't an easy way.

I plop the letter on the counter and stand beside him. "We need to talk."

His hands hover over the keyboard as his fingers jab at the keys. A moment later, he stops and looks down at the envelope and then up to me.

"What's up?"

"Open it," I say.

"I just need another minute—"

Sliding the envelope closer, I repeat, "Open it."

He huffs and pulls out the letter and reads it over. "Oh."

"I found it taped to the door last night when I came home."

"Oh," he repeats.

"That's it?"

He shrugs.

"Cale, what did you do? Who did you talk to? You've obviously pissed off the wrong person."

"Yeah. I'll be more careful, though. I'm done interviewing people—"

"You should drop this story completely," I urge. "Or take a different approach. It could get you killed."

"It could make my career!"

"And that's more important than your life?"

"This story needs to be told," he says. "The developers behind this project are working for the Martellis. I found, through unconventional means, that Leon Wallace himself deposited money into a bank account at the First Olympian National Bank downtown."

My mind flickers to the first corpse found there and my interest is piqued.

"What do you mean 'unconventional means'?"

Cale turns back to his computer. "Doesn't matter."

I shut his laptop. "Cale, come on, I'm serious."

He looks put off. "Let me remind you that only a couple weeks ago *you* were sticking your nose in places it shouldn't have been. Apparently your bruises didn't last long enough."

Not having a retort to his comment and being curious myself, I ask, "Whose account is it?"

"Exactly! That's what I've been looking into for the last week, but I finally found it. The account belongs to a Harold Pesti. But he's not a real person."

"What do you mean?"

"He has no driver's license, no social security number, no

address." He ticks them each off on his fingers.

"Then how does he even have a bank account?"

Cale shrugs. "I don't know. But I got to thinking. If Harold Pesti isn't even a real person, then why is there a bank account in his name? Somebody hiding money, probably. Someone who doesn't already have an account at that bank. Otherwise, the tellers would recognize him and wouldn't allow him to withdraw from the account."

"How do you know this person's not just depositing?" I ask.

Cale shakes his head, a smile across his face. "They're not. Or rather, money is being withdrawn in some fashion. ATM, check, never an over-the-counter withdrawal."

"I take it you found out whose account it really is?"

He nods. "The very question I wanted to answer when I first started this was how the project passed the environmental review. It's full of chemicals and completely uninhabitable in its current state. So I pulled the inspector's report for the site."

"Who was the inspector? Wouldn't that answer your question?"

"Yes, but the report claimed that Montgomery Works followed proper protocols for disposing of the chemical waste, which is bullshit. Anyone who's visited the site knows that. Thomas Davison, however, claimed everything was peachy."

"He's the inspector?"

Cale nods. "Uh-huh. And guess who—according to footage provided by a gullible security guard—makes frequent trips to FON Bank without having an account?"

"Davison?"

"The one and only. And guess where FON Bank's ATM is?"

"Inside the building?"

He nods. "I just need to get actual proof that Wallace is the one who deposits the money."

"You mean something credible?"

"Mm-hmm."

"Where did you hear about this bank account?"

"One of the workers down at the Works told me. Said Wallace pays him a couple hundred for each run to the bank to deposit money. As long as he never talks about it. Guess Wallace's money can only go so far, because the guy was an open book about it after I told him I'd pay him double."

"With what money?"

He wrinkles his nose. "Uh…the money I've been saving for Myra's engagement ring."

My eyes grow large. I didn't know Cale had been saving for an engagement ring. What's worse is I'm shocked that he would use money earmarked for that to pay off someone who works for Wallace.

"Cale…"

He holds up his hand to silence me. "I'll earn the money back when I get the inevitable promotion once this story goes public."

That's not a well-thought-out plan. Cale's usually more careful than that. He must be getting desperate now that he's close to uncovering the truth. But that likely means he's also getting sloppy, and that's concerning, especially after the letter. For the time being, though, I let it slide and continue with my questions.

"How do you plan on getting proof that Wallace deposited the money?" I ask, fearing the answer.

"I'm going to wear a wire and see if he'll fess up to it."

"Cale, that is incredibly stupid." I wave the Black Hand letter at him. "This is your proof! This is all the proof you need to realize you're making a horrible mistake! You said it yourself, the Martellis are behind this. Remember what you told me last month about them?"

"Ethan, I'll be fine. I'll go down and talk to Tucker and tell him about the letter. Maybe he can help me out and have a few officers on standby when I go to talk to Wallace."

I roll my eyes. "They're not your personal bodyguards."

"I'll be careful. I'll wait a little bit for this Black Hand stuff to die down before I pursue it some more."

"Good. Maybe then you'll come to your senses."

He ignores me. "I can't wait too long. Construction starts in the spring."

Chapter Twelve

I haven't been the new guy at work in a few years. I thought I had grown out of the nerves, but I guess you never do, because they are eating me up as the elevator climbs higher. I'm sandwiched between a woman in a maroon skirt who's scrolling through her phone and a large man who's breathing very heavy. The guy by the door in a UPS uniform snaps his gum as he watches the lights blink for each floor. I feel like I can't breathe. Finally, the doors open to my floor and I step out.

Through the window in the elevator lobby, I can see the shadows of the high-rises stretching across the metro area. The view helps puts things into perspective. Each of the three million people in the metro area have their own set of problems. At the moment, my apprehension about starting my new job pales in comparison. I smooth out my tie against my stomach and take a deep breath. I can do this.

Pushing through the glass doors into the open office space, I approach the front desk. There's a group of people discussing what I assume is their Thanksgiving holiday. They're each nursing a cup of coffee.

"…to my mother-in-law's," one man rambles. He's wearing a loose-fitting gray dress shirt with the sleeves haphazardly rolled up. "She makes the best stuffing. Jodie tries to make it, but hers never turns out."

"Nobody really ate stuffing at our house," says a woman in a brown sweater seated behind the desk. "I way overestimated how much food we needed. I was giving it away!"

The group laughs until I step up.

"Can I help you?" Brown Sweater asks curtly.

"Um…I'm Ethan Pierce. It's my first day."

"Have you done your orientation yet?" another woman asks. Both of her hands are huddled around a coffee cup.

"No, I don't think so," I reply to her.

"What's your position?" the man asks.

My mind goes blank and I pull out my phone to try to look it up. "Um…something with software development."

"Who's your supervisor?" he asks.

I blink. "I don't know." What was I saying about being able to do this? "The only person I talked to was Mr. Rizzoli."

Each of them give me disbelieving stares.

"*Frank* Rizzoli?" the woman at the desk asks.

I nod. "Yeah."

The three of them notice something behind me, and I turn to see Rizzoli step from the elevator.

"Ah, Mr. Pierce, nice to see you," he says with a smile. "Are you getting all settled in on your first day?"

"Um, actually—"

"I was just going to get him started with his paperwork," Brown Sweater says.

Rizzoli grips my shoulder and looks at her. "That can wait a minute, Sam. I want to give Mr. Pierce here the executive tour."

Sam nods while Gray Shirt proclaims, "That's a great idea!" and the woman with the coffee cup mutters, "I should get to work."

"Follow me." Rizzoli turns and walks farther into the office.

He leads me behind Sam's desk to one in the corner of the open office.

"This is where you'll be working, although you'll be running upstairs a lot to collaborate with the rest of the development staff."

Okay, so it's not my own office, but it's definitely an upgrade from the cubicle I worked in at Wyatt. My desk is even by a window!

He motions to the various items already on my desk. "You've got the desktop computer here. Most of the guys in development use theirs for the bulk of their work, but when you run upstairs, you can use this." I notice a silver laptop sitting next to the keyboard. "We can also get you a tablet, if you'd prefer that."

I nod wordlessly, trying to remember everything he's saying.

Rizzoli points to the office across the room. "Jackson Cowan is in that office. He's your supervisor, so you'll be working with him and the rest of the team a lot. If we can find him, I'll introduce you. He's been with us for about ten years now. He's actually the one who helped spearhead the first proposal before Mr. Moyer passed away and we lost it to Wyatt."

"Well, I'm excited to meet him." I place my keys on the desk.

"Oh yeah, make yourself comfortable. On the way upstairs I'll show you where the break room and everything is."

"This is all I brought," I tell him. I'm already the newbie; I didn't want to give reason for criticism by bringing in a bagged lunch. I know how offices can be. Very cliquey, just like high school.

He leads me back to the elevator, stopping at the break room and pointing out the bathroom along the way.

"I was surprised to see you at Thanksgiving," he says as we wait for the elevator.

"Yeah, Dean kind of told me about it the night before."

He smiles politely. "Still surprised that you two are so, uh…"

My face burns, and before I get a chance to correct him, the elevator doors open and we cram inside with the rest of the people going up.

Rizzoli's presence seems to silence everyone. He's the top dog, so everyone's on their best behavior.

He shows me the lab I'll be working in one floor up, the

employee cafeteria down on the second floor, and the conference room where we'll have department meetings.

"We'll probably have you jump in on one today," he tells me. "We just got the safety reports back, and there are some issues to clear up. Not to mention the bugs and troubleshooting we still have to do. We need you to be able to jump right in as soon as possible, so make sure you pay attention."

Oh sure, no pressure or anything. Maybe he's just playing with me, but his face is serious. It's all a little overwhelming, just like any new job is, but knowing what the circumstances were for me even being offered this position, I feel a little more stressed. Not to mention the cold reception I had when I first got here.

After the tour, Rizzoli brings me back to Sam to fill out my paperwork.

"You can fill these out in the meeting room over there, sweetie," she says in a tone very different from the one she used with me earlier this morning.

I wonder if the office knows what Rizzoli is involved with and that's why they're afraid of him. Although, I can attest for him being just plain intimidating. Good thing I'm on his side, then.

Taking the papers into the next room, I begin to fill them out. The usual new hire stuff. Just when I'm trying to remember the way I want to fill out my W-4, I hear my name.

"Are you Ethan?"

I look up and see a tall man with short, dark hair step in. He's wearing a crisp white shirt and black tie.

"I'm Jackson Cowan," he says extending his hand. "I'm the project manager for the solar roadways reproposal."

I shake his hand. "Oh, hi. Mr. Rizzoli told me a little about you."

"Nothing too horrible, I hope."

"Only good things, I swear."

"Well, I don't mean to interrupt you with the paperwork, but I just wanted to introduce myself. I reviewed your background with Mr. Rizzoli, and I agree that we need to get you started right away." He points to the ceiling. "We've got a department meeting upstairs that we'd like you to sit in on. Just to give you an idea of where we are and where we'd like to go so it'll be easier for you to jump in."

I nod, feeling my nerves return. I've never been involved in important meetings like that. My meetings at Wyatt were about new policies, safety training, or customer service etiquette. Never about anything that could change the trajectory of the company.

"Mr. Rizzoli told me a little about that," I tell him. "What time?"

"If you're done, I can take you up there right now and introduce you to everyone."

"Great."

After I drop the paperwork back with Sam, Mr. Cowan leads me to the elevator to go up to the conference room.

"I'll lead the meeting," he says as he types an email up on his phone, "then Jerry will give the financial report and Pearl will give the updated timeline report. We'll also have someone from software development give us a rundown of who's doing what. Then it'll be a brief question and comment section and we're done."

The elevator dings and we step on. Apparently my nerves are evident because he adds, "Relax, you'll be fine."

The room is packed when we walk in. Despite the long oak conference table being able to seat at least twenty, some people are still standing. They converse with one another while Mr. Cowan excuses himself to head up to the front of the room. I find a free spot against the wall and wait for the meeting to get started.

"Are you the new guy?" the large man from the elevator asks. His glasses are crooked and his curly hair is unkempt, but he seems friendly.

"Yeah." I extend my hand. "I'm Ethan. It's my first day."

"Brandon," he says. "First day and already jumping into a meeting, huh? They must really like you. Make sure to pay attention. They're going to put you to work."

I pat my empty pockets, suddenly realizing that I don't have a pad of paper or a pen or anything. Brandon notices and rips off two sheets from his notebook and hands them to me. "There are some pens up on the table."

"Okay, I think we're ready to begin," Mr. Cowan says loudly after I return to my spot standing against the back wall. "We have a lot to go over today, so please stay with me. First and foremost is welcoming our newest addition, Mr. Ethan Pierce."

The room fills with a smattering of applause and lots of smiles. Some of the guys standing next to me shake my hand and say, "Nice to meet you" or "Welcome."

"Ethan comes to us from Wyatt Industries and has an impressive background in software development and design. Mr. Rizzoli is very excited to have him aboard, so we should all give Ethan the same welcome.

"Now, to begin," he continues. "We're approaching the final stages of development: beta testing, implementation, and planning the rollout. Any bugs we find are going to have to be resolved fast. Mr. Rizzoli wants to present this to city council by the first of the year. That means we have less than a month to get this thing done."

Mr. Cowan runs down some of the things happening outside the office that need to line up with the completion of our software, like securing funding, ordering materials, and what areas of the city we hope to start with. After that, Jerry—a balding man with his last traces of hair combed over the top of his head—talks more in depth about the sources of funding and what the investors expect to see in the software. By the time Pearl finishes giving the updated timeline, Mr. Cowan reminds everyone of their responsibilities.

"Karen, we'll need the traffic pattern module from your team by the end of the week. Tom, get in touch with me about the specifics for the customer website. And Ethan, I'll have you jump right in to proofread and test some of the code that's already been written. Keep up the good work, everyone. We've come a long way, but we still have a lot to do."

After the meeting, Mr. Cowan leads me back down to my desk and gives me all my login information and shows me where

I can find the software code he wants me to review. Surprisingly, the amount of work that's required doesn't stress me out. I'm actually excited to get started. This is what I envisioned as my dream job since my first semester at OU.

More than that, though, this job sounds like it'll be different from Wyatt. I won't have a numbers quota to maintain, so the workload won't fall solely on my shoulders. It's a team effort—something we were sorely lacking in my department at Wyatt. Of course, dreams are often different from reality, but I'm trying to keep an open mind.

When I break for lunch, I notice I've got a text from Dean. *Good luck on your first day*, it says.

I smile because this looks like we're taking a step in the right direction, like we'll get past this and be friends. Who knows, maybe I'll meet a girl here at Tranidek who will be the one I end up with.

I reply, *Thanks! It's going well so far. How's work going for you?*

After my half-hour lunch break ends, I still haven't gotten a text back, which is disappointing. Can't say I'm surprised, though. He wants to be supportive, but I can imagine he's still upset. I guess, in some way, I led him on because I was afraid to tell him the truth.

Mr. Cowan sticks me with one of the tech guys to shadow for the rest of the day, which is a nice break after reviewing the code. All-in-all it's a very good first day. Not someplace I'll dread coming to. I'm actually looking forward to coming back tomorrow.

The elevator ride down to the main lobby doesn't feel like a suffocating box anymore. In fact, I can't seem to keep the smile off my face as I push through the glass doors out onto the sidewalk.

Three steps away from the building, though, I stop short as a skinless corpse falls to the sidewalk, splattering me with blood.

Chapter Thirteen

By time Tucker and some other police officers arrive, I already have a small crowd swarming around me. Someone hands me a towel for the blood, another person asks if I'm okay, and several people want to know what happened.

Tucker pulls me aside, and the other officers begin taping off the area. After another minute, I finally have space, but the police tape seems to draw an even larger crowd.

I wipe my face and halfheartedly wipe at my clothes. They're ruined. Just like my memories from my first day at work. Seeing the corpse land…I'm surprised my stomach hasn't turned yet. Must be that I'm getting desensitized to things like this. It was one thing to see one sitting on Dean's bike, but this was beyond brutal.

"Are you okay?" Tucker asks.

I open my mouth to respond, but the cameramen just outside the police tape distract me. My parents watch the news. Everyone I just met at my new job. I'll forever be the guy who was nearly crushed by a corpse.

The body lies ten feet away and is now covered by a tarp.

Still, the blood splatter brings back the vivid picture.

"I'm all right," I nod. "Alive."

"What exactly did you see?"

I shrug. "Nothing really. I was just heading home and it fell right in front of me."

He nods. "Did you look up to see if there was anyone there?"

Shaking my head, I say, "No." I glance up and see a few blood smears on the glass building. The body must've hit the side a couple times on its way down.

"Okay."

"Have you talked to anyone inside yet?" I ask. I wonder if this could get me fired for whatever reason. I'm sure nobody inside was almost crushed by a dead body on their first day.

"Ethan?"

I follow the sound of my brother's voice to the crowd. He wedges himself between two reporters, elbowing his way to the front.

"Ethan, are you okay?" he asks.

Taking a step toward him, I start to speak, but Tucker grabs my arm. Instead, he waves to one of the police officers manning the barrier line and Cale slips past and comes toward me.

"No camera, Pierce," Tucker says.

Cale ignores him and studies me. "Ethan, what happened?"

"I was just walking out and the body dropped."

"Are you okay?"

I nod.

"Did you see who it was?" he asks.

I shake my head again. "No."

He looks to Tucker. "Do you have any idea?"

"We're investigating all possibilities." Translation: no.

"Do you think it had anything to do with the first corpse that was found?" I ask Tucker. "The one downtown?"

Cale looks between me and Tucker. "Wait, this guy was skinned? I thought it was just a suicide jumper."

"This wasn't suicide," I tell him.

Cameras start to flash, and Tucker moves to block us from view as best he can. "I think I have enough from you for now. I'll be in touch if I have any other questions. Right now, though, I need to get in contact with some of the people inside. Come on."

He leads us into the building, where we sit in the lobby. Security has already put up privacy screens over the windows so no one can see inside. Still, everyone coming off the elevator looks our way before exiting on the other side of the building.

"Ethan, are you *sure* you're okay?" Cale asks. "You've seen a lot in the last couple months."

"No one was shooting at me," I say, "so I'll take this over what happened before."

"Ethan, you don't think it was…I mean, after the letter I got the other day…" His voice is a murmur. I need to strain to listen. "You don't think it could be Leon Wallace or Frank Rizzoli or someone?"

I have thought about Rizzoli, but why would he want to drop a body on my head? He just hired me. Unless Wallace was actually the one behind it, and he was using me to send a message to Cale. But then, why wouldn't he just drop the body in front of Cale? Unless he thinks that would expose him as Black Hand. And why pick such a public place? Just like the first murder, and I *know* Wallace didn't place that first body.

"I don't know, Cale," I finally respond, dropping my spinning head in my hands. Whoever it is, they're doing a good job of cleaning up their tracks. There has to be something around here that'd indicate it who it is. And it's my job as Fuse to find it.

———

I HAVEN'T TOLD Dean about the body yet. I meant to when I got home today, but he wasn't there. He never replied to my text asking where he was, so I think it's safe to say he's still upset with me. At the moment, I have bigger things to worry about.

Like, for instance, what the connection between the victims is. Since Carlo made the second body disappear, I can't look into that victim at all. I have to rely on the information I find from the other two, specifically the third body. That trail is still hot.

That's why I'm out here now, perched on the rooftop of the

Terrance Theater in my Fuse suit. I stare across the street to Tranidek Tower and try to figure out how the murderer got the body to the top of the building without being detected.

As I watch, I consider what Cale and Dean both said about Rizzoli. Even if he wasn't the one to drop the body from the roof—men like him probably like to keep their hands clean—he could've allowed the murderer up there. At the top of one of the tallest buildings in the city, nobody would spot him. But it still doesn't explain why he would put a spotlight on himself and Tranidek. And why would he want to drop a body on me?

Of course, this incident could be Rizzoli's way of exonerating himself. Still, it seems like a very risky move. But what if Carlo was right, and Bello is planning a coup? The first body could've been his way of sending a message to the whole city that he's untouchable, the second a message to Martelli that he's not safe, either. This last body was very clearly aimed for me. Although it's a risky move because it would draw attention—and it didn't exactly kill me—maybe a power play is exactly what Bello's going for?

But how would he be able to pull all of that off while in witness protection? He has to maintain a clean record in order to fulfill his end of the plea bargain.

My feet crunch in the snow on the roof tiles, and I shiver against the snowy wind. I need to move before the cold really gets to me. I wish I could get to the top of the Tranidek Tower, but I don't have my passcode yet. Even if I did, that would put Ethan Pierce at the top of the building when Fuse might very well be spotted heading up there. It wouldn't take long to put two and two together—especially not when I was the center of attention when the body was found. Besides, in this weather, I'd rather not go to the top of one of the tallest towers in the city. But then, this job is full of a lot of things that I'd rather not do. I guess I'll just have to see if I can investigate tomorrow during my day job.

When I turn toward the fire escape to get back to the street, something catches my eye. The glow of the downtown buildings illuminate the sky, and it takes me a minute before I see it again.

Light flashes just between two buildings down by the waterfront. It isn't until it flashes a third time that I realize it must be Myra. It's the same way she contacted me before.

I get back down to the street and jog all the way down North Main Street to city hall. Nearly two and half miles later, I'm there, breathing heavily from the brisk air. I curse my limited options for getting around the city and find the maintenance entry that I used the last couple times I was here.

Luckily, my breathing steadies by time I get up to Myra's floor. She's still on the rooftop outside the window, flashing the spotlight around.

Peeking my head out the window, I mutter in a deep voice, "You can stop doing that."

She yelps, clutching her hand to her chest. "Don't do that!"

I smirk behind my mask. "Sorry." I stand back to allow her to crawl through the window and close it behind her. I note how she meanders through the office, purposely putting desks between us.

"I got a chance to pull the names you wanted." She pulls a manila folder from a drawer in her desk.

I step forward to reach for the folder, but she pulls it closer to her.

"Digging around for this information can be risky for me. I know I asked how I can help, but I need to be careful. Especially with the special election coming up."

I nod. "I understand and I appreciate this."

She studies me for a moment and then hands over the folder. "What do you need this for, anyway?"

Skimming the names, I don't recognize many of them. But the name Darryl Hutchins sticks out to me. I stopped his little drug operation in Ashland right after Emma died and I was avoiding Dean. Seems like Bello was branching outside of his territory. But if he ultimately wants to overthrow Martelli, why wouldn't he?

But Hutchins wasn't a gang leader. Not really. He was in

charge of three or four street dealers, but that was it. He didn't seem to have much authority when I ran into him. Besides, he's in jail now.

"I'm working on a case," I finally say.

She rubs her hands together to warm them. "Against Michael Bello?"

"Against a lot of people." I close the folder and wave it in the air. "Thanks for this. Please don't go looking into this further, though. It could cost you the election." I turn to leave, but she stops me.

"Wait!" She spins the gold bracelet around on her wrist as she studies me, considering her question.

"Yes?"

Finally, she shakes her head. "Nothing. We're even now, right?"

"Of course." I walk backward toward the door. "Thanks again."

———

THE ELEVATOR DINGS when I reach the top floor of Tranidek Tower the next morning. When I got in the elevator, I noticed Rizzoli's floor was the last option. There isn't even a "maintenance only" option for the roof. Possibly a suicide prevention method. Still, there has to be some way to get up there.

On the other side of the windows in the elevator lobby, a cleaning crew is wiping up the blood smears from yesterday. I wonder if Tucker ever found someone who saw the body go by on its way to the pavement.

Before stepping into the main office, I take a look around the lobby. Besides the entry for the elevator, there's a door leading to the staircase. I'll have to check it out on my way down. I can see the receptionist from here, but if I pass off using the stairs as taking the healthier option, maybe she won't take notice. I'm still new, so it's not like it would be a change in behavior.

"Hi there," she says when I step through the glass doors into the office.

I point the manila folder toward Rizzo's office. "I just need to talk to Mr. Rizzoli for a second."

Her smile fades. "Did you set up an appointment?"

Biting my bottom lip, I say, "No. But I swear, it'll only take a minute."

"You really should've made an appointment." She reaches for her phone. "Let me see if he's in. He's been very busy."

Her eyes flicker to the men outside cleaning the window. Makes sense. He's been doing damage control.

I watch the men outside scrub the window while she tells Rizzo there's a "young man" who wants to talk to him.

"He says he'll see you real quick," she says when she hangs up the phone.

"Thank you," I mutter.

Mr. Rizzoli is sitting at his large desk when I step through the door.

"Hello, Mr. Pierce." He flashes me a quick smile and goes back to whatever he's writing. "Are you doing okay after what you were subjected to yesterday?"

"Yeah. No harm done," I reply. "Physically, at least."

"Good." His head is still turned toward his desk as he signs more papers. "This has turned into a fucking nightmare for me up here."

I press on. "I just—I, uh, have some information that I was hoping you could pass off to your, uh, boss."

All morning I've been debating whether or not I should give the names I got from Myra to Rizzoli. The truth of the matter is, I don't want to see Martelli. I've now witnessed three skinned corpses, one nearly killing me. Someone's after me, and I'd be stupid to go right to the mob boss himself with this target on my back. Not when I have a connection right here at work.

And I don't want Dean to deliver this information because I don't want him to be manipulated into doing anymore favors for his father. Part of me wants to believe Dean would be strong enough to say no, but it's still better not to tempt him.

Rizzoli's eyes narrow and he motions to the leather chairs in front of his desk. "Have a seat." Once I'm seated, he continues in a low murmur, "I believe I told you that once you're an employee of this company, any talk of work outside of this office is off limits, correct?"

There's fury in his eyes. A warning. I can see why so many people are afraid of him. How he got to the position he's in now, both at Tranidek and with the family. I wish I hadn't come up here.

"Yes, sir." I look down at the folder in my lap.

"Look at me," he demands, to which I comply. "Appearances must be kept up. Not only that, they must be *believable*. Confidence avoids suspicion."

"Yes, sir. I'm sorry. I just didn't want to drop it off directly because I thought that'd be obvious and I didn't know—"

He holds up his hand to stop me. "You know where I live. In the future, if you're unsure, you can bring it to my home directly. But—this is important, so pay attention—always make sure that whatever you want me to have, that you give it to me directly. Same goes for anyone else. You can never be too sure these days."

I nod and worry whether I should've just risked it and met up with Carlo somewhere. "Yes, sir."

Waving his fingers, he says, "Let's see what you have, then. Is this the information on our protected friend?"

I hand him the folder. "Yes, sir."

How much can I say? Are there security cameras or recorders? Can the receptionist hear what we're saying in here? Better to take extra precaution and not say much. I've had enough runins with the police lately.

Rizzoli glances at the contents of the folder. "Where'd you get this from?"

"Uh, a contact at city hall." My throat goes dry, and I wonder how much he's going to push me for details. I should've just trusted Dean and had him give this directly to Carlo. Dean's the one who's supposed to be doing the favor, anyway.

"And you made sure that they understood this was all confidential?"

"Yes, sir. They won't tell anyone." At least I didn't say *she*.

Closing the folder, he stuffs it into his briefcase beside his desk. "Very well. I'll pass it along."

Without a proper indication that this meeting is over, but not having anything else to say, I nervously get up and step toward the door.

"Actually," he says, his eyes still on his desk, "there's something else I'd like to ask you."

Spinning on my heels, I turn back toward him. "Yes? Sir."

"You're friends with Councilwoman Myra Connors, right?"

Goosebumps prickle all over my body. Did he already figure out the connection? I only hope Myra doesn't go down on account of me. I'm the one who roped her into this. Or rather, Fuse is.

Still, I can't lie. Definitely not to Rizzoli.

"Yeah, she's my brother's girlfriend."

"Well, then I'm sure you've seen this." He looks up long enough to hand me a copy of the *Tribune*. There's a picture of her on the rooftop with Fuse. Right near the spotlight. *Witness claims Connors in collusion with Fuse.*

Damn it.

I should've been more careful. I can't let Myra suffer because of me. The accusation alone at this crucial point in her career could derail everything for her. Would she have been so brazen if she knew James Alexander is about to announce his candidacy any day now?

And who is this witness, the person who took the photograph? Do they work for the *Tribune*? Is that how it ended up on the front page so fast? What else do they know? About her. About Fuse. About me.

"You might want to tell you friend at city hall to stay away from people like that," Rizzoli says. "I suspect from his line of work that associating with him is dangerous."

Chapter Fourteen

When I check the news the next day at work, I'm disappointed to see it isn't any better than yesterday's. Worse, actually. The photographer apparently had multiple photographs of Myra and Fuse at city hall, and by the time I got home last night, they were all over social media.

I read some of the comments. Nobody had good things to say about either of us. A lot of people were concerned about Myra having a conversation with Fuse so late at night without any notification to the press or any other officials present. Looking at it through their eyes, it does look suspicious. A lot of people worried about the capabilities of Fuse—"How do we know he's on our side?" "What happens if he turns against us?" "What's the city's plan to control him?" Even though just as many questions are being raised about Fuse as they are Myra, she's the only one who will really be hurt by it because she's not hiding behind a mask.

This morning there was an article about the level of security in government buildings, and it was clear the photos were the catalyst. Cale told me at breakfast that Myra was reprimanded at work, but he didn't know any other details. After that, she re-fused to talk to anyone, including him.

I can only imagine how she's feeling. She was nervous when she gave me those names. Worried about how it'd affect her ca-reer. Likely second-guessing ever offering to help me. Now she must really be kicking herself.

The fact that I'm to blame for this negative attention she's getting makes me feel guilty. I shouldn't have let her get those names for me. I should've figured it out myself. But then, how else would I have gotten that information?

My brain is swamped trying to juggle everything. My new job, issues with Dean, Myra's upcoming election, Fuse. I'm not any closer to figuring out the puzzle of the skinned bodies. Yes-terday when I left Rizzoli's office, I was so wrapped up in what he told me about Myra that I went right to the elevator. It wasn't until I was three floors down that I remembered I wanted to check out the stairs. I managed to get off and climbed the stairs to the top. There is a door that leads to the roof, but it looks like it's alarmed and requires a key and passcode to open it. So again, there is a possibility that Rizzoli could've helped the murderer reach the top, but I'm still not sipping that Kool-Aid just yet.

On my lunch break, I pull up the *Tribune*'s website. "James Alexander announces run for city council," reads the top head-line. Immediately, I click on it and start reading.

Local businessman James Alexander announced his run for city council today. Sources say his campaign is backed by several city council members since photos were released showing Myra Connors, the interim councilwoman, at city hall with Fuse.

"Nothing's conclusive, but it's good to have a back-up plan," Mayor Eugene Banks said at Alexander's press con-ference this morning. "Mr. Alexander is exactly the type of person we need on the council. He's a lifelong Olympian, has started several businesses, and continues to donate his time to activities that promote community and the sus-tainability of our city."

Alexander says he plans to run on what he calls an "honesty platform," which includes complete transparency and open meetings.

"My door is always open," he said. "Any time a resident has an issue, they can talk to me and I'll take care of it."

Since Councilman Frank Lloyd's termination last month, Lloyd's assistant, Myra Connors, has been acting council member. A special election will be held by the new year to elect a new council member. So far, only Connors and Alexander have been announced as candidates.

This is really bad timing, but I can't help but wonder if it was done on purpose. Myra's position on the council is really shaky now. I have faith that she'll pull it off and win the election, but she's going to need to focus. She's perfect for the job.

I'm about to click off, but another news article catches my eye, "Connors' initiatives get lukewarm reception."

Documents presented at last night's city council meeting regarding Interim Councilwoman Myra Connors' proposed initiatives for the Hopman district were not well-received.

Programs such as a boys and girls club, little free libraries, and a neighborhood block party fell short with the rest of the council.

"These are all terrific ideas, but where are the neighborhood voices standing up for programs like these?" Councilwoman Gertrude Percy asked. "All we've seen since Councilman Lloyd's departure is increased gang violence."

Councilman Leonard Levite echoed her thoughts. "These programs are going to be a drain on city resources if the residents aren't actually going to use them."

Other initiatives proposed for the district include creating a Historic District along the Lincoln Avenue corridor and leveraging historic tax credits through the state to attract investors, as well as the complete elimination of the Manhattan Expressway.

"The expressway cut off the community from the rest of the city, and the district has slowly become a trash dump," Connors said during her proposal. "Hopman has been forgotten and neglected. It's time we change that for residents. They deserve it."

Councilwoman Connors agreed to refine her proposals, including a more detailed budget, and will present at the city council meeting next week.

Damn, that girl can't catch a break. She's trying her hardest to do right by her district, but it seems the city council has already written off that whole section of the city.

With only five minutes left in my lunch break, I shoot her a text.

Just read some of your ideas for Hopman in the paper. They all sound great! Let me know if you need help with anything.

I don't expect a response back. Especially since she won't even talk to Cale. He seems to think she'll get over it quickly and get back to work. I can only hope he's right.

———

AS I MEANDER through the slushy sidewalks on my way home, I can't help but smile at how my day turned out. This was the second day I worked with Mr. Cowan and his team trying to debug a glitch in the software. After spending the day scrolling through lines of code trying to find an error, I finally found the problem.

"Fantastic!" Cowan told me with a genuine smile on his face. "Ethan found the error in the signal coding," he announced to the rest of the room.

I got several comments from my coworkers like, "Nice job, new guy!" or "Glad we snatched you from Wyatt!"

Later, when I was working on writing a piece of minor code, Cowan placed a large blueberry muffin on my desk and said,

"For finding the error in the code. The other guys spent all day yesterday looking for that, so good job."

Better yet, not a single person mentioned the body that was nearly dropped on me. When I'm working, it's easy to forget how I got the job and who made it happen for me, because I love it. It's challenging and interesting and fun. Best of all, I feel like I'm really making a difference to better the future of the city. I wish Emma were still alive to see how well I'm doing, but just the thought of how proud she'd be of me makes me smile.

Cale texts me as I unlock the front door to the apartment building and says he's going to Myra's to see if he can cheer her up. As I climb the stairs to my floor, I wonder if Dean will be home. He was already asleep last night when I got in and was up before me this morning, so I never got a chance to talk to him. Today I'm going to have to.

He's sitting at the kitchen counter eating a bowl of cereal when I come in. I feel a weird mixture of relief at finally seeing him and anxiety about the conversation I need to initiate.

"Hey," I mutter as I head to my bedroom.

"Hi." He doesn't look at me.

I drop my bag on the floor of my room and close the door while I change. I try to come up with the best opening line to ease the tension. *How was your day?* He'd probably just grumble. *Are we good?* That implies that I actually think we're good, when I know we're not. *So…about that sex…* Yeah, no.

He's rinsing out his bowl at the sink when I return to the kitchen.

"That's all you're having for dinner?" I ask.

"I'm not hungry."

"Dean, come on. I know you want more than that."

"Cook for yourself for once in your life," he snaps before disappearing to the bathroom.

When he comes out a few minutes later, I throw the knife I just used to make myself a sandwich in the sink. It echoes loudly off the metal basin. I'm annoyed with how petty he's being. We're adults. Can't we have a rational conversation about this without sniping at each other? I thought we were moving on from the awkwardness.

"Are we ever actually going to talk again, or is this the way things are going to be between us?" I snap.

"Oh, now you want to talk?" He crosses his big arms across his chest. "What do you want to talk about? The fact that you keep sending me mixed messages? That *you* wanted to sleep with me and then told me it was 'just sex'? That you completely shut down whenever things get uncomfortable?"

"What about you?" I counter, completely ignoring my sandwich on the counter. I'm not hungry anymore. "You had no right to kiss me! I had just lost my girlfriend and you acted like it was a perfect opportunity to move in on me. As if I'd ever showed an interest in you before."

He motions to my room. "You seemed to like it last week!"

"Fuck you."

"No, fuck you. You're just scared because you did something 'gay' and you actually liked it."

"That's not what this is! I didn't—"

"Oh, so you're usually just this cold with people you sleep with?" he counters. "Do you have any idea how it felt when you blew me off like that?"

I cross my arms and take in a deep breath. He has a point. I've been jerking him around since he first kissed me, never saying one way or the other how I felt. But what am I supposed to tell him when I don't know myself? I'd be lying if I said it wasn't nice, but afterward it just felt so…wrong.

But maybe that's just in my head.

"Don't be so melodramatic," I say. Picking up my sandwich, I eat it without really tasting it.

"Melodramatic? Are you being serious right now?"

"I never said we were together!" I shout. "I thought we were just fooling around."

"I don't do that. It's different for me."

I roll my eyes. This is what I don't want. We're arguing like we're dating. Like we expect something from each other.

He studies me and then turns away. "Just forget it."

"Now who's the one shutting down?"

Whirling around, he gets in my face. "You really want to hear it?"

I set what's left of my sandwich down and meet his eyes. "Try me."

Dean's chest heaves as he stares at me. I can see him swallow, but still the pained expression is on his face. He walks into the living room and takes a seat on the couch, facing away from me. I don't move, suddenly realizing he's serious. After the way I've been treating him, I don't think he wants me to follow him, but I need to say something.

"Dean, if it's that personal you don't—"

"It was just after my mom died," he says quickly. "My father heard from one of his guys that I"—he clears his throat—"that I kissed another boy from school. Nothing bad, just a peck on the lips." He picks at the calluses on his hands. "But that was enough for my father. He was pissed. Embarrassed, I think, mostly. Said Mom would be disappointed in me if she were alive."

All I can manage to do is stand silently and stare at the floor. For the moment, I let the friendship and relationship boundary blur so that Dean can talk.

"He kicked me out. Nobody would take me in. Word spread throughout the family what I…what I'd done. I dropped out of school. Had to start begging people for money, food, anything. Each day I wondered where I was going to get my next meal from, where I was going to sleep, *if* I'd sleep. Whether I'd even still be alive in the morning. Men like my father…they hate people like me. It's not beneath them to stab someone in their sleep. Or worse."

"How long?" My voice is a croak.

"A few weeks. Maybe a month or two at most. That's when Jamie Alexander found me. He didn't even recognize me at first. I was begging outside his bakery. He owned so many, I didn't even know it was his. He said I could come back to his place and he'd give me something proper to eat. Said a Martelli shouldn't be on the streets begging for food like an animal.

"I was grateful. Jamie was a good friend of my father's, and

I knew he was risking his rank in the family by helping me." He pauses and looks out the window at the dark sky. "I would offer to do the dishes, cook, whatever needed to be done around the house. I figured it was the least I could do for him letting me stay."

He shakes his head. "Then he started making requests. They started out as jobs for the family. Those became more intense, but at his house…" He sighs. "He would spill his whiskey or whatever on my shirt and then demand that I wash it right away. I only had a few sets of clothes, so I'd be walking around without a shirt until the laundry was done."

My mind buzzes as I figure out where this is going. All I want is to just slam on the brakes. Make it stop. Make it so it never happened. But Dean goes on.

"Eventually he'd insist on helping me change. Said I was clumsy and that he had a lot of antiques. One day, my clothes were missing. I swear he hid them. No other reason they'd be gone, really. He told me a real man should be comfortable enough to walk around naked. I tried to argue, but he said he'd throw me back out on the street if I didn't listen. Said he'd tell my father where I was and that I came on to him. My father would've killed me."

"Dean—" I mutter in a thick voice.

He ignores me. "Things escalated from there. Touching me, telling me to do things to him…recording it." He wipes at his eyes. "Every time he'd cross that line, he'd remind me that I had no choice. That if I didn't want to live on the streets, I needed to do what he said.

"The first time he"—he waves his hand, struggling with the words—"forced himself on me, I thought he'd be done. He'd gotten what he wanted, and I thought I would be old news. But it happened again. And again. Almost every day."

He buries his face in his hands as the tears come, and I move to the couch and rub his back. I wrap my arms around him, wishing that this was just a dream.

"When I got arrested, that was my saving grace. I got out. I got away from Jamie. I never saw him again. Until last week."

I hold him tight, resting my head on his shoulder and forgetting all of my worries. They don't matter right now. Nothing does. Only him. "Dean, I'm so sorry that happened to you."

He pulls away from me. "You were the first person I…was with since him."

I close my eyes as the guilt crushes me.

"I always told myself that the next time I was with—the next time I had sex, that it'd be different." Finally, he meets my eyes. Besides the tears, he looks reproachful, and it hits me like a truck. "Guess I was wrong." He wipes at his face and stands.

On my feet, I reach for him, try to pull him back on the couch. I can't take back what I said, no, but maybe I can convince him that I do care about him. That I'm sorry for what I said.

"Dean, wait," I grab hold of his arm and pull him back toward the living room. "I'm sorry. I should've thought about what you were feeling. I was being selfish."

Grabbing his coat, he pulls out of my grasp and walks to the door, giving me a sad look just before he leaves.

Chapter Fifteen

Despite wanting to run after Dean to make sure he's okay—and to apologize for the way I acted after Thanksgiving night—my instincts tell me to let him go. Let him be alone for a little while. Chasing after him will only build his resentment toward me. I have to talk to him about it again tonight, though. Letting it slide will only tell him that I don't care about him or what happened, and that's just not true.

In the meantime, I need to distract myself. I pull out my computer and take a seat at the kitchen counter to start looking into information on the third body. There has to be news on it, now that there's a pattern. I especially know that because I know there were victims. I just need to put the clues together to figure out who's behind them.

Still, my mind wanders to what I just learned. I bite at the fingernail on my right thumb. I can't stop thinking about what he told me. A teenaged Dean, desperate and vulnerable. His whole world changed by a horny pervert.

James Alexander. He's still free. I knew something was off about him at Thanksgiving. He and Dean didn't act like two old friends who had recently been reacquainted. No, Dean looked terrified. Traumatized, really. And who could blame him? If I knew then, I would've…

I need to focus. Get back to my research so there aren't any more victims. I spit out a piece of my fingernail that I managed to bite off and bring my attention back to my computer. The *Tribune* still hasn't posted anything on their website about the third body, other than the fact that it was found and that I was nearly taken out about it. Apparently, "the man who was struck by lightning" is a good enough description of me.

I'm sure Tranidek is loving the fact a photograph of the blood smears on the side of the iconic building accompanies the story. Every company would *love* to have a corpse fall off its roof. Then again, not every company is linked to the Martellis.

It makes me wonder if Carlo knows what really happened between Dean and Alexander. Does he care? He seemed genuinely happy to see Dean last week, so I can't imagine that's the case. But some people have a funny way of reacting to news they don't want to hear. Like when Carlo found out Dean kissed a boy. Or when Alex asked me if Dean and I were dating…

If Carlo knows, he's pushed it out of his mind so far he barely thinks about it.

My back is knotted up from hunching over my computer and I've successfully chewed my fingernail down to the cuticle. Any farther and it'll start bleeding.

Since the *Tribune* has nothing, I consider my other options. There's Myra, although she probably doesn't know any more than I do. I could ask Tucker, but what story would I tell him to explain why I'm so interested?

The thought of Tucker, though, leads me down another path. It's potentially dangerous, but what else is new?

My fingers fly across the keyboard as I punch in strings of code, first to protect my identity, then to get into the OPD server. I've already set all of this up at the clinic, but the apartment is quiet, and I'd rather not field questions from Alex and Wes right now. Besides, protecting this computer won't take me too long.

Predictably, there are several layers of firewalls I need to get through before I can access any of the information I need. It takes awhile, only because I have to wait for my computer to generate the correct password for me to plug in. Another fingernail chewed off.

Finally, after nearly twenty minutes, I'm in. Now the searching begins. I have no idea where the files would be held, but I've hacked into unknown servers plenty of times before and usually found what I needed. I'll just have to keep searching until I find it.

My leg bounces on the rung of the chair as I click through different files and folders, ignoring the fire in my back. After many failed attempts, I finally uncover a group of files labeled "Skinned Murder Victims."

I skim through the file on the third victim and see that he's been identified as Perry Jonas. Again, the name doesn't ring any bells. I write it down and other pertinent details and check out the list of suspects. Not surprisingly, Carlo Martelli is at the top of the list. Probably because of the cruelty of the murders. These men weren't just killed, they were mutilated.

Michael Bello's gang leaders from the list Myra got me are also listed, as well as Joe Gotti, who first told me that Rizzoli wanted to talk to me. Back when I was still doing interviews after I was shocked. That seems like a lifetime ago.

Maybe I am biased toward the Martelli family, but besides Joe Gotti and Carlo Martelli, the rest of the names seem like long shots. And I'm still not convinced Martelli is a viable suspect, either. Not with the way he acted at Thanksgiving under the pretense that Dean and I were together.

I Google some of the other suspects, out of sheer curiosity. Most were either previously arrested for hate crimes or detained while disrupting gatherings meant for gay rights supporters: the pride parade, the LGBT center, or other public gatherings.

Another quick search on Google tells me exactly who Perry Jonas is. *Tribune* articles reading, "Jonas says Midtown Pride Parade will be bigger this year," "Jonas asks council to consider new bathroom policy," and "Olympia Pride Fest celebrates marriage equality" fill the first page of the search results.

Fuse: Omertà

At the top of the results, though, is Jonas's website. His "About" page says he's a "public speaker" and his talks have all been about LGBT issues.

Under Pressure: Deciding when you're ready to come out

Shifting Views: How the idea of the traditional family is changing

Societal expectations of gay men

His name and his talks both draw blanks for me, but his other work is certainly recognizable, specifically the annual Pride Parade he plans in the Midtown Theatre District every year. Not only that, but it looks like he routinely traveled to other cities to help organize other such events.

As active as he was in fighting for gay rights, from what I've found, he lived a very normal life. He and his partner owned a townhouse in the Fruit Belt—a wealthy neighborhood, but certainly not the richest. Based off of pictures on Facebook, it looked like they had a dog and traveled a lot.

One post from his partner particularly stands out to me. It was posted last night. *Come home* with a frown emoji. The comments all ask what's wrong, but he doesn't respond to any of them.

Searching through his list of over a thousand friends doesn't bring up any familiar names at first, until I stop on Lee Howes, the first victim. Clicking on it, I search for images of them together. The only image I find is way back in June—at the Pride Parade.

I pull up Howes's profile. Sifting through the pictures, I see one of the filters used from June is the pride flag. I'm willing to bet the second victim was there as well.

Pushing aside my computer, I grab my phone and text Dean.

Think I figured out the connection between the three bodies that were found. They're targeting us, Dean. Call or text me. Please.

Chapter Fifteen

Getting up from my seat, I dig through the junk drawer by the fridge and pull out a pad of paper and a pen. At the top, I list all of the information on the victims I know. The first body was found outside the First Olympian National Bank downtown with a newspaper announcing Bello's plea deal. The second was on Dean's bike at his father's house, posed like he was riding it. The third was simply dropped from the top of Tranidek Tower in front of me.

I hold my pen on the last period at the end of the list as I read it over. It's almost like the first body was presented for both me and Dean, since we were both on the rooftop of the Stanley Hotel when we found it. The other two bodies were meant for me and Dean separately…but we were together at Carlo's house.

Maybe the perpetrator knows we're together—or have been together intimately.

Sex, Ethan. Dean and I had sex. I need to get more comfortable with that fact.

Anyway, after our cold reception at Thanksgiving dinner, the murderer could be any one of Martelli's men. I start to list the top suspects in the right corner of the pad of paper: Carlo Martelli right at the top. Flicking my pen against the pad, I study the list.

I don't think Martelli would allow an attack on an outsider. Technically, Dean is out of the family business. He's off-limits, right? Even if he wasn't, why would Martelli target us after he asked us for a favor? And I even delivered!

Carlo Martelli's name gets crossed off.

Next on the list is Michael Bello's gang leaders, but I'm worried I'm only considering them because I'm mad Bello's no longer locked up. And would he even be able to pull something like this off—three times, nonetheless—while in witness protection?

Their names get crossed off too.

The one who makes the most sense is Frank Rizzoli, but would I still have a job if he's no longer there to justify my position to the board? Sure, I already started working, but I haven't been there long enough to prove my worth yet.

That's a selfish reason, I know. If Rizzoli is the murderer, it's my responsibility to bring him to justice. I circle his name a couple times, but I'm still not convinced.

The question remains: Why would Rizzoli want to kill these men? He followed through with my employment even after Dean and I went to Thanksgiving dinner together. Although, he had strict orders from Martelli to give me the job, but he seemed just as friendly on my first day. That was, until I brought up criminal business at work. Then he turned cold.

Maybe Martelli has someone at Tranidek's office as a messenger to verify that Rizzoli was following through with his promise. Once the mole was no longer in the office, Rizzoli had no reason to hide his disdain for me. Did one little misunderstanding cause all of this?

Of course not, the first body was found *before* Thanksgiving. Whatever hatred Rizzoli might have developed toward me and Dean after seeing us together wasn't there when the first victim was killed. Either the murderer is someone else or Rizzoli would have a different motive besides hating gays.

That trips me up for a long while, and I scribble notes at the bottom of the pad to try to figure it out. Meanwhile, the minutes keep ticking away without a word from Dean.

I type out another text to him, but erase it and lock my phone again. If he's not ready to talk, then I can wait. I set my phone down and chew on the end of my pen.

No, I need to be there for him, whether he likes it or not. Even if he doesn't answer, he has to know that I'm thinking about him. That I'm worried about him. That I care about him.

I pick up the phone and call him, still biting the end of the pen as it rings.

No answer.

I hang up without leaving a voicemail. I'll try again in a minute.

As important as it is to finally figure out who the murderer is and develop a plan to get him arrested, I can't help thinking about what Dean told me earlier. The abuse he endured while living with Alexander. The trauma he must've gone through when he unexpectedly saw him at Thanksgiving. That could send even the strongest person into a tailspin.

Picking up my phone again, I redial Dean's number. If I want to show him I'm here for him, asking him for help on something unrelated to what he told me seems like the perfect option. If nothing else, hearing his voice will give me peace of mind that he's okay.

The call goes to voicemail so I send another text: *I really need you to call me.*

I get up to get a glass of water, but I can't keep my hands still. Something's wrong. Which means Dean's in trouble. Whether it's from himself or someone else remains to be seen. Would he be desperate enough to kill himself? It seems like if he lived through the hell Alexander put him through, he'd be fearless to everything else. But then, I can't relate to where his head is. Not at all.

I try calling him one more time, but it goes to voicemail again. I search through my contacts and call Alex right away.

"Hey," she answers. "I haven't talked to you in a while. I was hoping you'd call. How are you?"

"Hi," I stammer. "Has Dean been down to the clinic at all tonight?"

"No, I haven't seen him," she says. "But about that…I actually wanted to apologize for what I said the other day. Whether you and Dean are together is none of my business. I'm just trying to look out for you, and your loyalty to him didn't make sense to me so I was jumping to conclusions."

What a time for an apology. I barely register it as I consider other places Dean might be. "It's fine. If you see him or hear from him, please let me know."

"Ethan, what's going on?"

I shake my head. "Nothing. He's just not answering my calls."

"Is he in trouble?"

"I don't know." Best not to worry her just yet. Not until I cover all my bases.

"You make me nervous with him."

"Yeah, I know."

She lets out a deep breath. "But I suppose I have to trust your judgment on him."

Ordinarily, this might've brought a smile to my face, but I'm really only half listening. My mind is too consumed with what-if scenarios and wondering where Dean might be.

"Thanks, Alex. Look, I have to go. I'll call you if I need anything. If you hear from Dean, call me right away."

"Sure. You know where I am."

I click off without saying good-bye and press my fist against my mouth. Dean usually answers his phone when I call. Granted, he's never been this upset before, but it still seems odd.

My mind goes to the images of the skinned corpses. Most of their distinguishing features ripped off, their bodies mutilated. Only someone filled with true hatred could do that to someone.

Thinking of truly evil people brings me back to James Alexander and what he did to Dean. That took pure evil to consistently take advantage of someone like that. Only someone who has been desensitized to violence would be able to strip away someone's skin. Someone in Martelli's business.

I decide to dig into Alexander's history. Although the mafia is very big on not writing anything down, everybody has a past. I'm determined to find it.

He has no Facebook account, no Twitter, and no recognizable email address other than the one for his office. He'd be stupid to have any sort of incriminating evidence there, but I check anyway. If this man is a pervert, he's going to have some skeletons in his closet. There must be a secret email address or an account somewhere he uses for his sick sexual fantasies. I doubt he stopped with Dean.

Unfortunately, I don't find any secret addresses, but since his work email is hosted by Gmail, I'm able to hack into his search history. Even if Alexander's not the murderer, I'd love to put him away for something. Other victims, child porn, anything.

At first glance, his search history is pretty normal. Searches for places to eat, random words—likely to check spelling—currency conversion. The only thing that stands out is a search for a site called InterPERVonals.

Chapter Fifteen

Clicking on it brings up a series of firewalls that I need to hack through to get in. I make sure to add as many protections to my computer as I can. It takes me awhile and my leg bounces nervously as I wait for my computer to catch up.

Once I get through, my stomach turns at what I see. It's a forum website where pedophiles encourage each other to rape children or offer tips on how to keep it hidden. There are even posts stating they contain images of children. "Girl, under ten," "Boy, early teens," even "Baby." Swallowing the bile in my throat, I press on.

Using Alexander's email, I log in in to his account. His password is the same as his email password. Idiot. Putting my blinders on as much as I can, I look through only the posts Alexander contributed to. Luckily, his aren't too bad in comparison.

He mostly starts his own threads and doesn't respond to many others. A lot of his posts are from years ago, likely around the time Dean was living with him, but I try not to think about it. I don't want to taint my image of Dean with what happened to him. I don't want to be reminded of Alexander whenever I see Dean.

Alexander's words are poetic, but they don't really say much. A desperate plea for attention, if you ask me. Then again, I'm biased.

Some days I feel like a monster is trying to get out. Break my ribs and emerge.

I wish life were simpler. It's so hard to want something you know you're not supposed to have.

Shameful. That's me in a nutshell.

The few responses I read through are disgusting. Other perverts making excuses for their actions by talking about their "needs," completely oblivious, either willfully or not, to the pain they're inflicting on their victims.

I kind of want to burn my computer after this. I hate it that these kinds of people exist in this world. In an effort to get off of this website as quickly as I can, I skim through the rest of Alexander's posts, looking for anything that stands out. Some of them are more straightforward, discussing the actual things he's worrying about.

I know my father would be ashamed of me and the person I've become. No conviction. No purpose. I'm forever in his shadow because I've never been brave enough to step out from behind him.

My father died today. Laid down for a nap and never woke up. I would say that I miss him, but that would be misleading. Not when I finally found that conviction he wanted to see in me.

It's amazing how my father still has an impact on me even though he's gone. Still the reason I cry at night. Still the reason I hurt myself. Probably even the reason I'm like this.

I'm disgusting, just like he said. The family name will die with me because I'm not man enough to take a wife.

Bingo. James Alexander is gay, which comes as no surprise after tonight. The fact that he hated himself for it, though, that's something. Might even be exactly what I'm looking for. I remember the disgusted look he gave me and Dean when we held hands at Thanksgiving.

In fact, it makes even more sense now. Alexander has a reason to attack gays. Twisted, absolutely, but a motive nonetheless.

Scrolling back to the top of the page, I click the most recent entry, which is from last week.

Been a while since I posted here. I'm a changed man. Truly, I am. No longer the scared boy I was then. Now, I'm the person my father would be proud of. Still not married,

Chapter Fifteen

but at least I've renounced my former temptations. Better, actually. Today, I took a step forward in making sure that anyone who was like the way I used to be no longer walks in this city. I may not be able to take care of them all, but I can definitely make it known that this city is not a place for fags.

Chapter Sixteen

I sit at the kitchen counter panicking. James Alexander is most definitely the murderer. Not only that, but he's fixated on Dean.

Reaching for my phone again, I redial Dean's number. No ring, just straight to voicemail.

I can't believe this is happening again. Someone else I care about is in danger. I have to find him. If something happens to him, I won't be able to live with myself. What am I doing as Fuse if I can't even protect the people closest to me? With all the power that I have, I should be able to do *something*.

Pulling my laptop to me again, I punch in the code to get into the Grid. Plugging in my phone, I use the signal from the last call I made to Dean's phone—when it actually rang—and backtrace it for his location. Looks like he's on Broadway near Wilkinson Avenue.

Or rather, *was*. God only knows where he is now.

Wait. I might actually know where he is. Jumping to my feet, I pull my clothes off as fast as I can and slip on my Fuse suit, replacing my clothes over it. I grab a bag and stuff my Fuse boots into it and head out the door.

Not wanting to waste time getting a cab, I run the distance to Dean's apartment building and anxiously wait in the shadows for someone to enter with their key fob so I can follow them in.

When I finally make it up to Dean's floor, I put my ear against his door and listen for anything inside.

Nothing.

I jiggle the handle, knowing full well that it's probably locked. Still, I need to make sure that he's not in there.

God, I hope he's not in there.

With adrenaline running through me, I kick the door once, twice before it gives way and I step through. The stench is worse now, and I notice more flies swarming in the bathroom. Must be what's left of one of the other victims. I pay it no mind and search the room.

There's no one here, although the blanket is pulled back from Dean's bed in the corner and the weapons are missing. How Alexander got them out unnoticed is beyond me, but right now that doesn't matter.

Dean's still gone and I have no idea where he is.

I pull up Alex's number again and call her.

"Need something already?" she asks with a giggle.

"I need your help." My voice quivers with fear. Worry.

She becomes serious. "What's wrong?"

"I think Dean's in trouble. I can't get ahold of him, and now his phone is dead." I run my free hand through my hair and tug at it a little bit. Try to wake myself up from this nightmare.

"Why do you think something's happened? Maybe his phone just died."

"Maybe, but I don't think so. I've already wasted enough time. I waited too long with Emma before, I can't do that again."

"Slow down. What are you talking about?"

"I need your help, Alex. Please?"

"Okay," she says softly. "What do you need me to do?"

"Do you remember how to pull up the traffic cams using the Grid?"

"You mean break into whatever system you did last time? No."

I groan.

"Wes might remember, but I think he has an event tonight at OU."

"Dammit."

"I'll call him, though," she adds. "What are we looking at, exactly?"

"I'm not sure yet. See if you can get Wes and get down to the clinic. I've already encrypted that computer so it's harder to pinpoint if you get caught hacking."

"What are you going to be doing?"

"I'm going to talk to Dean's father."

———

I CONSIDER LOOKING for Dean in the spot where his phone last pinged, but when my cab passes by there, I realize there's no way he'd still be around. It's a well-traveled intersection for cars, trains, and people. If he was abducted there, someone would have seen. His phone must've been dropped from a passing car.

Instead, I direct the cab to Carlo Martelli's house. Unlike when we came at Thanksgiving, the entry to his dead-end street is blocked by two men in suits. They eye the cab carefully as it pulls up.

"Right here's fine," I mutter to the cab driver as I hand him a wad of cash. "Thanks."

The men look more intimidating up close. One of them has his hands crossed in front of him, concealing a gun.

"What's your business here?" the other one asks.

"I need to talk to Carlo Martelli."

"He's not expecting visitors," he responds.

"I know, but it's about his son—"

"Get out of here," the one with the gun says.

"Please, could you just ask him? It's really important!"

"Go!"

They each grab my arms and drag me backward toward the parkway. I could resist—Dean showed me how—but I know it'll only make matters worse.

Chapter Sixteen

"He could be in serious trouble! I know who's been dropping the bodies! I need Carlo's help to stop him!"

The men let me go and look at each other.

"What bodies?" the one with the gun asks.

If these guards know anything about me, it's that I'm with Dean. Telling them the murderer is targeting gays isn't going to persuade them to let me see Carlo. I need to make it personal. I need to make it about them.

"The skinless ones that have been found around the city." I fix my shirt. "Each of them near a member of the Martelli family. First Leon Wallace, then Carlo himself, and finally Frank Rizzoli."

The men eye each other until the one without the gun turns and pulls out his phone. He steps away to talk into it, and I can't make out what he's saying. A minute later, he turns back to us and says, "Come on."

They escort me up the street right to Carlo's front door. Such a stark difference from the last time I was here, when Dean and I just walked up.

I'm taken aback when Frank Rizzoli answers the door.

He offers a slight nod. "Mr. Pierce."

"Hi," I mutter.

Rizzo looks back at the men and steps aside for me to enter. Once he shuts the door behind me, he leads me to the office off the dining room in the front of the house.

"Have a seat." He motions to one of the two seats in front of the desk.

"This is important. I need to talk to Mr. Martelli."

"Whatever you have to say to Mr. Martelli, you can say to me."

Can I trust him? Somehow James Alexander got the last body up to the roof of Tranidek Tower. Was Rizzoli the one who gave him access?

Either way, time is ticking and I need to figure out where Dean is before it's too late. I can't lose him too.

"I don't have time for this." My voice rises. "Let me talk to Carlo Martelli. The longer we wait, the greater the chance is that

Dean's skin will be peeled off and his body dumped somewhere. Just like everyone else."

"Well," a voice says from the doorway, "that certainly got my attention."

I turn and see the boss himself.

Mindful of the traditions of the Martelli family, I say, "Sorry for being disrespectful, sir. I'm just really worried."

Carlo turns to Rizzo. "Frankie, if you wouldn't mind."

Rizzoli eyes me and then steps past Martelli, shutting the door behind him.

Slowly, he steps behind his desk and looks out the window. "What's been on your mind, Mr. Pierce?"

I dive into the reasons why I suspect James Alexander is the one who has been dropping the bodies. The pervert forum, the post alluding to his sexuality, and his promise to kill other gay people.

"Based on the way he reacted when he saw me and Dean here at Thanksgiving, I have a feeling Dean is the next target," I finish.

Carlo's quiet for a long while, likely choosing his words carefully.

"Mr. Alexander has been a longtime friend of this family," he says with a stern look. "I have no reason not to trust him, other than the story you're spouting now. Pardon me if I have my hesitations about the authenticity of your theory."

His face turned to disbelief from the moment I told him that Alexander was gay himself. Is Martelli's acceptance of his son a lie to get Dean closer? Why would he do that? What does he need Dean for? Another recruit?

At this moment, though, it doesn't matter. I need to find Dean. I need Martelli's help. I need to convince him I'm right. Fast.

"I have the link for the entries Alexander left online—"

He turns to admire the map on the wall adjacent to the windows overlooking the front yard. "Tricky thing about the internet, isn't it?" he says, cutting me off. "You can be whoever you want to be."

I shake my head. "No, this is him. It all makes sense."

"I think it's best you leave now." He steps around the desk toward the door. "Frankie can show you the way out."

"Wait!" I shout.

Carlo turns and I once again have his attention. Dean would kill me for this, but if it's the only way to save him, I have to do it.

"Dean told me that you kicked him out when he was a teenager."

He fixes the lapels on his shirt. "Yes, and as I've since shown this past week, I no longer hold such a strong stance on that topic."

Based on his reaction to Alexander's outing, I'm not sure if I believe him. But I press on.

"But not everyone is ready to change," I continue.

He doesn't say anything but continues to study me.

"Dean said Alexander was the only one who took him in after he spent time living on the streets."

"Mr. Pierce, I'm growing tired of this conversation."

"Dean told me about the circumstances of that situation. How Alexander got…friendly with him. Made him do things." I swallow my nerves and add, "Sexually."

Based on the color draining from Carlo's face, it was the right call to really get his attention. Still, he's silent and I don't know what his next move will be.

"James Alexander has been killing gay men and leaving them at the footsteps of *your* supporters," I continue in his silence. "It must be his way of showing you that he doesn't want to accept people like De—people like *us* into your group."

Carlo's jaw clenches.

"Please, Mr. Martelli. I know things between you and your son are complicated, but believe me. I care a lot about him. I don't want him to get hurt."

Carlo leans against the edge of the desk. "When he asked to leave the family business, he mentioned something about Jamie, but I just thought—I never imagined…" He shakes his head.

"I've already been to Dean's apartment. That's where Alexander has been carving up his victims. There are still…remains of the others." I shake my head and try to keep the worry out of my voice. "Alexander and Dean aren't there. I have no idea where they could be."

The legal address for James Alexander is next door to here. But as protected as this street is, I very much doubt that's where he's holding Dean.

"James owns a rental house. Uh, 1411 Allen Street." Carlo's voice is hollow, and he stares at the floor as he speaks. "He's renovating it for new tenants, but it's empty right now. Used to be his parents' house. It's where Dino stayed when…"

I feel a lump forming in my throat. The things that must be going through Carlo's mind right now. The things that could be happening to Dean right now. I have to get there as quickly as I can. I have to get him out of there. I need him safe.

"Thank you. I'll hurry." I turn to leave, but Carlo stops me.

"No, wait. My men can get in there without bringing the police into this. You go home. I'll take care of it." He starts toward the door, but stops when I don't move. "Is there a problem?"

"No. I can't just go home. I want to help." I force myself to keep my voice steady against my rising fear.

"Mr. Pierce, I can assure you that if things are as gruesome as you claim, you do not want to see Dino in such a state." He puts his hand on my shoulder. "Go home. Someone will be by later to tell you how it went. You have my word."

He gives a slight tug that tells me to get walking to the door, with which I'm forced to comply. I don't have any more excuses to argue otherwise. And honestly, Martelli and his men would hold me back. Especially since they don't know I'm Fuse.

Martelli walks me to the end of the driveway, where one of his guards meets us.

"Milo here will get you a ride home, if you'd like one," Martelli tells me.

I shake my head. "No, that's okay. I'll walk."

They exchange glances before Martelli turns back to me and says something I never thought I'd hear him say.

"Thank you, Mr. Pierce."

I nod. "Of course."

As I follow the guard down to the end of the street where I was dropped off, I can't help but worry that I'm wasting time. I can't sit by idly while Dean is being—

Dean's tough. He should be able to fend off Alexander long enough until his father's men get there.

But what if he can't? What if it's just like what happened with Emma? I have to get to him. I have to do something. I've figured out this much already. I'll be able to take out all this frustration on Dean's abuser. It would do us both some good.

Nodding slightly to the guard and trying my best to walk casually down to the next street—knowing that they're likely watching me—I find a nook in between the shrubbery between two houses once I'm out of sight of Martelli's men.

In the darkness of the night, I quickly strip down to my Fuse suit and stuff my clothes in my bag. With one last look around, I slip out from the bushes and take off in a run toward 1411 Allen Street.

Chapter Seventeen

The address Carlo gave me is an end unit in a series of row-houses. I creep through the darkness of the alley to get to the house undetected. My black Fuse suit helps keep me hidden. It's perfect for late-night excursions like these.

On the way over here, I called Alex again to see how she was doing with the traffic cams. Not so well, according to her. Apparently Wes couldn't get out of his plans tonight. I'm annoyed but I can't be mad at him. He signed up to research me, not be my wingman. Alex isn't the most tech savvy, so I can't expect her bring up the traffic cameras and, honestly, I'm not sure they'd be much help anyway if we're inside Alexander's house.

Instead, I told her to record whatever she hears over the com. I'm hoping to get some sort of confession out of Alexander so he can be locked up.

In the meantime, I locate a small open window at the base of the house and quietly lie on my stomach to look inside. It looks into the basement, and my blood boils at what I see. Dean's wrists are bound to the floor joist above his head, and his toes just barely drag on the ground. Worse, he's completely naked.

My mind races, trying to figure out my game plan, trying not to think about what Alexander might've already done to Dean before I got here. Not only was Dean recently reacquainted with his abuser, he's completely at his mercy again. In the same house from before.

Seeing Dean like this makes me shake with anger. He looks so tired. Drugged, perhaps. Like the three other guys before him, there's no way he can get out of here on his own. He needs me.

Pulling my eyes away from Dean, I take in the rest of the room. Large buckets sit in the corner next to an old refrigerator spotted with dents and stains. The pile of Dean's clothes lay to his right.

What really catches my attention, though, is the table full of knives and other sharp instruments. The same ones we saw at Dean's apartment. A box of latex gloves sits in the corner of the table. Wouldn't want to get any blood on our hands, would we, James? The bastard probably thinks gay man's blood is poison or something.

A thick wooden support beam obscures my view of Alexander, but I still spot two stone skewers sticking out from a base on the table. I can hear the swiping of the metal against the abrasive edge of the skewers as he runs a knife along each, sharpening the blade.

I stretch out my arm and try to get a clear shot to tase him. I just want to knock him out long enough to get down there. Then I can get the confession out of him.

With the beam in the way, I can't get a clear shot of him. I need to figure out how to get inside without zapping him first. Getting the confession is important to putting him away for these murders. To get justice for the torment he put these men through. James Alexander needs to be imprisoned.

I'd also love to see him put away for what he did to Dean all those years ago. The guys in prison will take care of him for that.

First thing's first, though: getting down there so I can actually do something without any obstructions. Making sure not to make any noise, I reach for my phone in my bag and snap a few pictures. I try not to get Dean in them, but I have to include him in some. It'll help exonerate Dean since Alexander was previously working out of his apartment. Besides, showing Alexander committing the crime is important to putting him away. I just wish I had a better shot of Alexander's face. Still, I can't wait to get them off my phone as soon as possible. I don't want to remember this.

Just as I'm about to get back to my feet to find a way inside, the sound of Alexander's voice stops me.

"You know, we've been here before Dino, haven't we?" he says. The steady rhythm of metal sliding against stone continues.

Dean's silent, but Alexander presses on.

"Not quite the same way. You were eager before. But that was a long time ago. You've grown to be quite the young man. Still loyal to the family that raised you, the people who took you in." He chuckles. "I have to be honest, I miss your companionship, but the way you manipulated me to do those…*vile things.*" He shakes his head. "I thought you changed, just like I have, but then you brought your…*man friend* to Thanksgiving. It sealed your fate."

Alexander's words stir Dean.

"*I* manipulated *you*?" His voice is thick, sluggish. He picks up his head, but his eyelids are still heavy.

"You were a different person then, Dino. Angry at the world because of Patty's death—"

"Keep her name out of your mouth!" he shouts.

The sound of metal on stone stops and Alexander clucks his tongue. "Still so full of anger. You see, Dino, I found you at a rough spot in your life. I tried to help you."

"You made my life hell."

"Giving you a place to stay and feeding you was hell?" He shakes his head. "Once you got comfortable, you took advantage in a way that I never expected from you. You're lucky I never told your father."

"My father got over it. You saw that last week."

"Oh, Dino, my boy, your father is humoring you. He wants something from you. The same way you'd pretend to be the good boy in public all those years ago. But at home, you wrapped me up in your disgusting habits."

"You said you'd tell my father I started it if I didn't…" Dean's voice is shaky and I worry he's starting to believe Alexander's manipulation.

"You *did* start it, Dino. I was the victim."

"No, I remember the first time. In the shower. I felt—"

"Enough of your sick sexual fantasies!" Alexander shouts for the first time, pointing the knife from across the room. "You know that's not what happened."

Dean doesn't reply.

"I know for a fact that you liked it."

That's enough. I need to get down there, but if I try to open the outside basement door and discover that it's locked from the inside, Alexander might just shove that knife right through Dean's heart to speed things up.

I try the back door instead since it's farther away and will make less noise if I can't get through. It's open, but the door squeaks when I enter. Behind my mask I cringe and brace myself to shock any attackers, but none come. Alexander's voice carries from the basement—still trying to convince Dean of his story—so I know they haven't heard me.

The house is gutted. The studs are the only things resembling walls, and I can see all the way to the front door. I assume from the pipes jutting up from the floor that I'm in the kitchen, but there's nothing else to indicate that. Tools are piled around a wooden ladder to the side, but other than that, there's nothing else in the room.

The basement door in the corner sits ajar. Alexander's voice carries from below. I have no idea what my plan of action is. If I go down the stairs, I'll be completely exposed. I only saw knives in Alexander's collection, but he could be concealing a gun on his person. I'd be no good to Dean if I got shot.

But what other choice do I have? I'm fresh out of options.

Pulling open the door in the kitchen farther, I lean forward, trying to get a sight line of Dean before I run down there. I don't want to accidentally hurt him during this. I search for any other weapons, but like the rest of the house, the basement appears to be pretty bare from the vantage point I have.

"Since we have a history, I'll ask if you have a preference where I start," Alexander says to Dean.

I see the flat side of the blade run against Dean's bare stomach and move down to his thigh. No cuts yet. Alexander's teasing him.

"The leg usually feels less pain, but the skin is so thin," he continues. "Especially as fit as you are. There's nothing to really…grab on to." I can almost hear the smile in his voice.

His hand clutches ahold of Dean like he's property, and that's when I move. Halfway down the stairs, I throw my arm out to the room, shooting a short burst of lightning from my palm. Nothing deadly, in case I hit Dean. Luckily, it hits Alexander and he falls to the ground.

"Oh, thank God," Dean mutters when he sees me. His chest heaves as he breathes in a shuddering sigh.

I snatch the knife from the concrete floor where James dropped it and wedge it between the ropes around Dean's wrists.

"We're going to get you out of here. You'll be fine. We just need to get you free, and then we can put this bastard away." I feel the need to fill the air with positive thoughts. I made it. I'm here. Nothing is going to happen to Dean. After we take care of James, it'll be just the two of us and—

"Ethan!" Dean shouts, his eyes fixated behind me.

Before I have a chance to look, I feel the blunt force against the back of my neck.

The world goes dark.

Chapter Eighteen

The pain wakes me up. My neck, my wrists, my head—everything throbs, and my senses are dulled. It isn't until I take a deep breath and open my eyes that I realize James Alexander and his bad combover are inches away from me. A yellow-toothed grin spreads across his face.

"Just in time for the show." He moves over to Dean and presses the knife against his skin. "Think of this as an orientation. If you'd like, I'll walk you through each step."

Dean looks more sluggish than he was before. Alexander must've given him a second dose of sedative.

"James, don't do this," I shout. "We didn't do anything to you!" I hope someone outside hears me. I don't even care if they know I'm Fuse. I just need to do something. I need to get Dean out of here.

My lightning ability won't work since my hands are tied up to the rafters. Whatever energy I muster would be shot up at the ceiling, potentially caving in the house and hurting all three of us.

Keep him talking, that's the best I can do for now. With any luck, Martelli and his men will get here before Alexander hurts either of us.

I don't know what's taking him so long, though. Even if he had to round up his men from their houses, he should've been here by now. I wonder if he ever planned on coming. Worse, I wonder if he's using Alexander to do his dirty work.

No. Carlo was genuinely shaken when I told him about Dean. He wouldn't do that to his own son. No matter what he's done in the past, he's still a father. Even if he did throw Dean out all those years ago.

"I tried," James says. "I really did. I took young Dino here in. Gave him a home, food, a warm bed. And what did he do? Ran into the arms of a *man*."

"From what I've read, what you really want is to run into the arms of a man too," I tell him, stalling.

His head snaps to me. "Watch your mouth!"

He lifts the knife and cuts me quickly on my cheek. It stings, but there are worse things he could've done. Still, I feel the blood run down to my neck.

Returning to the table, he talks to me with his back turned. "You people are disgusting. It's supposed to be a *man* and a *woman*. It's simple biology. It's how God intended it. Carlo, of all people, was the one to understand that."

"Carlo doesn't seem to have a problem with it anymore," I say.

He snarls, "I know." Turning back around, he approaches Dean. "I was so proud to be a made man after Carlo disowned Dino here from the family all those years ago."

His hand cradles Dean's cheek, but his eyes wander down his naked body.

"I still think we should've killed him—as we do with men like you two—but it was hard enough for Carlo to lose his son so soon after he lost his wife. His only son. What a disappointment he turned out to be."

"So why start the killing spree? Dean never contacted you. Why would he after—" I stop myself. Alexander wants to rewrite the history of what happened. Arguing with him about it when he's the one with the knife in his hand isn't going to get us any-where.

"After what?" He smiles. When I don't say anything he continues, "You'll have noticed on your way in that the house is in the process of being remodeled. My former tenant was a man like yourself. Keep in mind, I use the word *man* loosely."

He waits for my reaction, but I don't have one for him.

"Anyway, I obviously didn't know that when he first moved in. Not until I dropped by to talk to one of the contractors inspecting the roof. That's when I discovered his…his…"

"Boyfriend?" I say for him.

He glares at me. "Yes. I couldn't have that. All the haunted memories from when I was so badly taken advantage of came back to me."

I fight the urge to roll my eyes. "So you lured him to Dean's apartment and killed him?"

"Not my tenant, unfortunately, no. When I came to do the deed, the only one home was his…"

"Boyfriend?" He can't even say it.

He smiles. "You know, it's amazing how much pain the human body can sustain. Slip them a few sedatives and go to work. Of course, despite the pills, they still sometimes wake up. By then, I've usually got a good start in removing their skin. It's always a relief when the screams stop. Not just for the quiet, but to know that I finally got through to them."

"Why remove the skin? Why not just kill them?"

He looks at me like I should know the answer.

"It prepares them for the pain they'll experience in eternal damnation. Ethan, it's only going to get worse from here. Your judgment day is coming sooner than you think."

Lifting the knife to the center of Dean's chest, he presses the tip of the blade in and I shout incoherently. With any luck, I'll wake a neighbor or something. It's late, but it's my only move.

He pulls the knife away. "Is there a problem?"

A trickle of blood runs down Dean's front from the gash.

"Why did you pose the bodies where Martelli's men could find them?" I ask. "Why not just tell them you don't want Dean rejoining because…because of me?"

"So many questions."

"If you're just going to kill me, what does it matter?"

He studies me a minute and then says, "The bodies were displayed to remind the Martellis what we do to men like you. Kill them. I used the opportunity to not only eliminate more men like you, but also to send a message to the Martellis that we must stick to the traditions that bind us. Plus, there were some, like Dino here, that I liked to play with a bit."

I bite my tongue. Is that what he did with Dean before I got here? Is that why he's naked? How can Alexander continue to deny that he's attracted to men? Like Dean? Like us?

Like me.

"Uh…" I have to keep him talking. "What about the newspaper? The one about Michael Bello's release?"

"Ah, that's part of a master plan you won't live long enough to see." He turns back to Dean and repositions his knife.

"Carlo thinks he's planning a coup!" I yelp.

"I'd be disappointed if he didn't suspect something of that nature." He ignores me and buries his knife deeper into Dean's chest and drags it down. "He's a very intelligent man."

"You're helping Bello overthrow Martelli, aren't you?" I'm spitballing here, desperate to say something that will get the blade away from Dean. But the more I talk, the more it makes sense. "That's why you never told Martelli that you don't want Dean to rejoin. So others would turn on him too. It's why you're targeting Dean right now, to shove it in Carlo's face. It's even why you're running for council, to counteract the influence of Martelli's contacts at city hall. I'm right, aren't I?"

Alexander throws his arm to the side, sending the knife in my direction. The sharp blade grazes me, cutting a hole in the stomach of my suit and slicing a surface wound on my skin.

"Shut up!" He drives a punch to my stomach that knocks the air out of me. "This is *exactly* why I do this to you people! To show that you're inferior."

Retrieving a new knife from the table, Alexander returns to Dean.

Chapter Eighteen

"Why do you think I'm letting you watch?" he asks as I struggle for breath. "You care for this man, don't you?"

I swallow my rage down as my chest tightens. "Yes."

"Then the pain will be double for you, and I'll have the added satisfaction of seeing your spirit die along with your body. Now shut your mouth and let me get to work."

I can't pull my eyes away, but I don't want to watch, either. Blood trickles down from where he struck me with the knife, but it's nothing compared to the blood covering Dean from the long, deep cut Alexander carves into him.

My fear takes over and I shout, "Stop! Please stop!"

Alexander ignores me when his knife reaches just above Dean's belly button. He slips it in his back pocket and reaches toward the bleeding cut.

There's a commotion upstairs and Alexander stops. He grumbles and removes his gloves, tossing them in the bucket by the fridge. Pulling a gun from the waist of his jeans, he looks at me and whispers, "Keep quiet or I'll shoot you both."

I nod, just to get him to go away, grateful to watch him disappear up the stairs.

"Dean," I whisper-shout.

Nothing.

"Dean," I try again.

Still nothing.

Looking up, I grab ahold of the rope holding me to the rafter, pull myself up, wrap my legs around the rafter, and hang upside down. With my muscles straining and the blood rushing to my head, I wiggle my wrists as much as I can inside the restraints. The knot was tied so that as I hung, I tightened it. Now that my body weight is no longer hanging from the knot, it begins to loosen.

Finally, I'm able to slip out my right hand. I quickly pull at the rope and free my left hand. I drop to the floor, stretching out my shoulders.

As I move toward Dean to free him, the commotion upstairs grows louder, and suddenly James Alexander comes tumbling down the stairs.

Chapter Nineteen

The room is still for a few moments and I wonder who is upstairs. Are they going to try to kill us? Would I be able to take them down? Should I hide until they come downstairs? What about Dean? Indecisiveness freezes me in place.

Slow footsteps descend the stairs, and Carlo Martelli steps into view. Ironic how I'm grateful to see him when just a few weeks ago I was terrified of him.

"James drugged him," I tell him as I move to Dean's side. "We need to get him to the hospital."

Carlo grabs a knife from Alexander's table of weapons and reaches for the rope that binds Dean's wrists.

"I need you to hold him," he tells me. I nod my acknowledgement and wrap my tired arms around Dean's waist as his father cuts him free.

I nearly fall to the floor from the weight of Dean's body, but I manage to stay on my feet. Carlo drops the knife and pulls his son from me, cradling his head.

"My boy," he mutters.

Despite all the power Carlo Martelli wields, the things he's done to friends, strangers, even his own family, deep down he truly does care for Dean. There are no tears, but the gentle way he strokes Dean's face shows it.

Behind Carlo, I notice James Alexander stir. Without a word, I wave Carlo out of the way. Half dragging his son, they move farther into the basement.

As I watch Alexander get to his feet, I kick Dean's clothes toward his father. If he can get him ready to run, maybe I can stun Alexander. It'd be easier to kill him, but I don't know how much energy I have after being tied up. Besides, death is nothing compared to the lifelong turmoil he triggered in Dean.

Alexander flashes his yellow-toothed smile. "You little prick."

Pulling one of the ropes down from the rafter, I say, "Your plan didn't work, James. Turn yourself in."

He reaches back and pulls the bloody knife from his back pocket and lunges at me.

Hopping back, I let electricity crackle between my fingers. He swings at me again, knocking my forearm.

"Out of the way!" Carlo shouts from behind me. He has a pistol aimed in our direction. Dean lies on the ground, still bleeding, although his father managed to get his lower half covered.

"No!" I turn my head and shout. I want Alexander locked up for what he did to Dean all those years ago. I want—

I take a blow to the head and crumple to the ground.

A gunshot fires, but my vision is blacked out. When my eyes do focus, I see Carlo against the far wall, holding his jaw and Alexander pointing the gun at me. My ears ring from the blast of the gun.

"You're going to keep your little lightning bolts to yourself while I finish with your boy toy," Alexander sneers.

Breathing heavy and still dizzy, I stare at him. I'm not sure if I will have accuracy to zap him. But if I'm going to do it, it has to be before he lays his hands on Dean again.

As Alexander moves down to Dean, my eyes flicker to Carlo. He gives a slight nod before grabbing Alexander around the waist and pulling him away from Dean. They scramble on the floor for a minute before Alexander jabs his knee into Carlo's gut and backs away on his hands and knees.

Sneaking up behind him while he points the gun at Carlo, I put my hands on either side of his head. Along with my fury, I release all my pent-up energy out of my palms and into Alexander. It only takes a few seconds before his body goes limp.

Carlo and I exchange looks but don't say anything for a while. After a moment he nods over to Dean. "I have a car out back waiting to take us to the hospital just down the street," he tells me, referring to St. Mary's Hospital. "Get Dino out of here. I'll be up in a minute."

Hoisting Dean up, I wrap my arm around his waist and shuffle to the steps. His feet drag on the ground, but still I manage to get up two steps.

I nearly fall backward, however, when two gunshots fire again. One right after the other.

The pistol in Carlo's hand is pointed directly at Alexander's chest. He pauses and then fires three more shots into his chest.

Though my ears ring, I see the anger on Carlo's face as he crosses the room and takes his position on Dean's other side. He helps me pull him up the stairs and out the back door to the car without a word between us.

Two men approach us as we exit. Carlo points back to the house and says, "Get rid of the body and wipe the place clean. My son is not going to prison for this."

Once we get Dean seated, I run back to the basement window and snatch up my bag and return to the car. The door is barely shut before it's pulling away. Joe Gotti is behind the wheel. He keeps his eyes on the road as he directs us to the emergency room.

"Here." Seated in the front passenger seat, Carlo passes me something black.

My mask.

"There'll be people at the hospital, so…" He looks out the window but doesn't say a word.

Quietly, I pull my regular clothes over my Fuse suit. As I pull on my pants, my leg kicks Dean's and he stirs again.

Chapter Nineteen

"Wha—Ethan?"

"I'm here," I tell him.

I reach for his hand and squeeze again, though I try to hide it from his father. James Alexander couldn't have been the only one in Martelli's entourage who didn't approve of me and Dean. I don't want to risk it.

Me and Dean.

After everything that's happened today—from Dean's confession to almost losing him to Alexander—the thought of us as *us* doesn't scare me anymore. I need him. I care about him. Feeling awkward about it doesn't change the fact that I want to be with him. Completely. I've finally admitted it to myself.

"How are you going to explain Dean's injuries?" I ask quietly.

Nobody says anything for a while. I begin to think nobody heard me, but finally Martelli speaks up.

"Let me handle that."

I wonder if he's going to admit that Dean was Alexander's next victim. That would explain Dean's injuries but raise a number of other questions. Especially now that the police are equipped with Michael Bello's information on the family, I'm not sure Martelli would put himself at the scene of the crime. As we pull into the hospital parking lot, the fact that I have bigger things to worry about at the moment fill my mind.

The doctors take Dean back right away when we bring him through the ER. Carlo's presence alone seems to stifle questions and speed up the process. Luckily, I've only ever been a patient at the hospital downtown, so nobody recognizes me here.

I take a seat in the waiting room while Carlo leaves to talk to Gotti. Probably giving him further instructions for damage control. The gunshots were loud. It's the middle of the night in a pretty safe neighborhood. The police are likely already there. I wonder if Tucker is among them.

Carlo comes back in and takes a seat in the chair next to me in the nearly empty waiting room. I don't know what to make of him or what he thinks of me, but I'm sure he'd rather keep a sense of mystery about himself. Won't let anyone know what he's thinking.

Through the window, I can see one of his guards standing in the vestibule. Carlo has eyes everywhere, that's for sure.

"I'm not a man who is usually lost for words," Carlo starts.

He pauses and I wait for him to continue, wondering where he's going with this or if he expects me to say something. The leader of the Martelli crime family knows I'm Fuse. He can make me his bitch for however long he wants to.

"I've seen a lot, and not much surprises me anymore," he finally continues. "But the way I saw my son today…I can't describe it."

I play with the button on my shirt. "Yeah, it was bad."

"Believe me, I've seen worse. Strangers, enemies, even a few former friends. But Dino." He shakes his head and press a finger to his chest when he says, "*My* son."

Another long pause. I'm a basket case right now, worrying about Dean's recovery, waiting for the other shoe to fall with my secret exposed to Carlo, and reeling with my admission to myself about my desire to be with Dean.

"I wasn't sure if I believed what you said about Mr. Alexander," he goes on. "But my men went to Dino's apartment, and it was like you said. I couldn't take that chance with him."

Not sure what to say, I don't say anything.

"Mr. Alexander had every intension of killing him, didn't he? The both of you, actually."

In a small voice, I say, "Yeah."

"And you stopped him. You saved my son." He offers his hand. "Thank you."

Shaking his hand, I finally look him in the eye. I open my mouth to say something, but he continues.

"Oh, and make sure to pass along a thank you to your friend Fuse." He raises his eyebrows and then looks away.

"I will, sir." I wonder how often he thanks people for disobeying him.

We're quiet again as I take in his words. Despite my best efforts, the events of the evening play like a loop in my head, starting with Dean's confession. One thing sticks out to me, though.

"Sir, if you don't mind me asking, what took you so long to

get to the house?" Even if Carlo did go to Dean's apartment first, it wouldn't have taken him that long to get back to Allen Street. Especially not in the middle of the night.

He frowns. "There was an issue that required my immediate attention. I wish I could've come sooner, but luckily you were there."

I don't know what he's talking about at first and then I remember the names I asked Myra to get. "About Bell—"

His brow creases and he shakes his head slightly. "Not here. I have an idea where my former friend might be, and I intend to catch up with him."

"So what does this mean for…?"

"For you and my son? Consider yourselves free men. I expect, however, that you'll uphold our code?"

Omertà. The vow of silence, even as you're standing in the flames. Until me, Dean's kept that vow. I don't see why I wouldn't either. Carlo helped save my life tonight. And Dean's. As he would say, I owe him a favor.

After I nod my agreement, our conversation dies off, and I watch the movie playing on the TV in the waiting room, but my attention is elsewhere. Halfway through, a woman in green scrubs with a black stethoscope around her neck approaches us.

"Are you two waiting for Mr. Adams?"

I nod. "Yeah. How's he doing?"

"Very well. He's still a little groggy, but his vitals are strong and he's all patched up."

"Can we see him?" I ask.

"I'm sorry, family only."

Carlo puts up his hand. "This young man is family."

The weight of those words sits heavy on my shoulders. At the moment, though, I don't care. I just need to see Dean.

He's asleep when we get to his room. Likely a mix of the drugs Alexander gave him and the local anesthetic the doctors gave him. I don't blame him. My eyes are heavy and I'm ready to put this night behind us.

I take a seat in the chair beside him and watch as he breathes. If I learned anything from losing Emma, it's that I need to spend more time with the people I care about. I'm not going to make the same mistake with Dean.

As my eyes begin to droop, Carlo clears his throat to get my attention.

"I can give you a ride home if you'd like."

I shake my head. "No thank you. I'd like to stay here."

"He's in good hands with these doctors. And I'll have someone watching the door at all times."

"I know. But I'd still like to stay."

He nods. I can tell he still has reservations about me and Dean, but he doesn't voice them. Instead, he shakes my hand one more time before leaving.

After Carlo leaves, I sit back in the chair and get as comfortable as I can. Before I give in to my heavy eyelids, I take in Dean's sleeping form. He's healing but healthy, which brings a smile to my face. We did it. We stopped James Alexander from hurting anyone else and finally put Dean's demons to rest.

Taking his hand in mine, I kiss the back of it, feeling the immense sense of relief now that he's safe.

Chapter Twenty

How do they feel?" Alex asks Dean as he unbuttons his shirt at the clinic. We're in one of the exam rooms and he's sitting up on the medical table with his shirt open while Alex checks out his stitches. I'm leaning against the small counter, still so happy that everything turned out.

"Tight," he says. "But otherwise good."

His skin is still puffy, but the stitches are holding up nicely. The hospital released him this morning. Other than being groggier than usual, he seems to have bounced back.

"How do you think they look?" he asks.

Alex lets out a deep breath and rocks her head back and forth. "Still a little swollen, but just keep dressing it and you should be okay. Ethan can help with that." She turns and smiles at me before returning to Dean. "Any limitations in movement? Trouble sitting up, stuff like that?"

"Not really. They said it didn't go through to the muscle."

She nods. "That's what I was thinking too. Let me put more bandages on so it doesn't get infected, and then you're all set."

Pulling some materials out of the cupboard next to me, she gets to work.

"You know," she says, "there's another reason why I wanted you to come in. I'm sure Ethan told you that I was here listening in on everything that happened last night."

I cringe. I didn't get a chance to tell him that yet, but he doesn't seem surprised.

"So you're telling me you're drowsy?" Dean's attempt at a joke falls flat as the humor doesn't quite reach his eyes.

We haven't talked about last night much. After we got home early this morning, he was so beat that he just went to bed. I still had to work today, so I didn't get that luxury. I haven't had the time—or the courage—to ask him what happened before I got there. I'm not sure I want to know.

"I'm very well-rested, thank you." She asks Dean to lie down so she can better adhere the bandages. "I recorded the conversation and got Alexander's comments about you two."

My cheeks flare up, and I stare at the ground. Another thing I haven't thought much about. Last night was the first time I accepted how I feel about Dean. Now someone's responding to what's only been in my head this whole time. I don't want to know what Alex or anyone thinks about it. It's still so personal.

What I'm most worried about, though, is how Dean will take it now that Alex knows about his abusive past. He went from nobody knowing to several people knowing in just one evening. I wonder if the circumstances will dull the pain for him at all. I'm not sure it would make a difference if it were me. I'd still be embarrassed that so many people knew.

"You heard, then," he mutters, keeping his eyes fixated on the ceiling.

"Yeah," she replies quietly, fussing with his bandages. She doesn't meet his eyes.

She pulls out a jump drive from her white coat pocket.

"I know he's dead, but the recording is all here," she says. "I think I deleted it completely from the computer downstairs, so this should be the only copy."

He takes it from her.

"Thanks, Alex," I say.

If she heard everything, that means she knows Carlo was there. It means she heard the gunshots. It means she knows Dean wasn't the one trying to hurt me.

I know she said she'd give Dean a chance, but I think last night—and the recording on this jump drive—helped push her in the right direction to finally start trusting Dean. She's probably still suspicious of his family, but so am I. My trust in Dean, however, is firmly intact.

———

DEAN INSISTS ON taking me out to dinner after we leave the clinic. As he puts it, I saved his life, so the least he could do is buy me a meal. It's actually a perfect setup for what I want to say to him. I finally have his full attention.

Chester Park Grill is a short walk from my apartment. The hostess seats us on the second floor near the large window that overlooks the park. The midtown skyline is visible in the background. The way the newly fallen snow coats the ground in the park, it's really a picturesque setting.

After we order, neither of us knows what to say to the other. Last night we connected—*really* connected—but it seems we both sobered up from our feelings overnight. Rather, Dean sobered up. I'm just getting a taste of what I've been putting him through. It sucks.

"Do you think you'll take time off of work?" I ask.

He shrugs. "I don't know, maybe."

"You're going to need time to heal."

"Mm-hmm." He looks out the window.

"So...what about your apartment? Did the police come and get your statement?"

"Yeah, while you were at work."

I nod. "Gotcha."

"Yeah."

If there's any suspicion that Dean was actually the one skinning those men, the recording on the jump drive will absolve him of that.

"If you don't want to talk about this, we don't have to."

"I'm fine." But he still doesn't look at me.

With nothing else to distract us, I take the plunge and initiate what I want to tell him. What I need to tell him.

"I'm sorry for the way I acted after we…" My chest is tight and I feel like I'm on fire, but I force myself to keep talking. "…slept together."

"Ethan, it's fine. You already apologized."

"If I knew what you'd been through—"

"Ethan," he cuts in. "Let's not talk about that."

"About what? What happened, or us?"

He lifts his eyebrows. "*Is* there an us?"

"Dean, you have to realize this is hard for me."

Finally, he looks at me and shrugs. "You're right. Sorry for that. I put a lot of pressure on you after Emma and—"

"I care about you," I blurt. "A lot. I was lying when I said it was 'just sex.'" I shrug. "I don't know. I guess you were right and I was just scared. This is not at all where I thought my life would end up."

His expression softens and he offers a sad smile. "I care a lot about you, too. I know it's hard. It's still kind of new for me, too."

I'm very aware of the fact that our hands are only inches away on the table. A part of me wants to reach for his, but I don't. Still, a wide smile spreads across my face.

"So, what do you say? Are we going to give this a try?"

Does that make Dean my boyfriend? It sounds so weird to say, but I've been telling myself it over and over all day to get used to the idea. It's so soon after Emma, but it feels right. Dean gave me a purpose after she was attacked and even after she died. He's been there for me, and I want to be there for him. This is as sure as I've been about anything since I was electrocuted. I want this. I want him.

"Ethan, I would love nothing more than to give this a try."

I reach for his hand but he pulls away.

"But…I don't think I'm ready. Not anymore."

"What do you mean?" The heat in my chest seems to drop to my stomach.

Chapter Twenty

"Seeing Jamie again…being tied up like that…" His shoulders raise into a shrug and he shakes his head. "I need to work through that. I haven't gotten over it like I thought I had. And the fact that it happened again… It's a lot to work through."

I nod, trying not to show how disappointed I am. It makes sense. How could I expect Dean to be ready to be intimate with someone when he was just reacquainted with his abuser? And after the way I reacted the first time we were together, I can't apologize enough times to make up for that hurt.

Suddenly, though, a fear strikes through me.

"When I got there last night, you were…naked."

He presses his fist to his mouth and looks away.

"Dean, did he…" I gulp. "He didn't…? Not again."

His voice breaks and he diverts his eyes from me. Staring out the window. "I don't know. I can't remember."

I can see he's fighting tears because his eyes are glassy. He presses his fingers against his eyes and sniffles.

"I have to use the bathroom," he mutters as he stands with his head down.

I watch as he meanders quickly around the tables to the restroom.

Whatever weightlessness I felt earlier is gone. I rest my chin against my fists and stare at the empty seat across from me while my mind runs wild.

I can't be upset with him for this. Bad memories—or worse, *no* memories. I suppose that's what angers me most. The unknown. James Alexander was a manipulator who was so good at it he even convinced himself that it was his duty to punish people he deemed sinful. Ignored the fact that he liked men too. Drugging Dean, taking advantage of him, and then lying about it was just another day for him.

I'm glad he's dead.

Pulling out my phone, I read through the *Tribune* article about Alexander's murders. The police found his setup in Dean's apartment. Hopefully Tucker comes to me or Cale to verify that Dean's been staying with us before they start suspecting him.

I don't think he'd be a suspect if he was one of Alexander's victims. Hospital records show that, especially if Carlo has influence over the staff. Hell, he can probably make it go away for Dean at the police station, too. After everything Dean's been through, he doesn't need a murder trial on his hands.

I read through all the updates on the *Tribune*'s website on my phone before I notice Dean standing beside our table. His eyes are dry but still puffy.

"Do you want to just go—" he starts, but my phone buzzing interrupts him.

I look up at him, silently asking if what he was going to say can wait.

He nods. "Answer it."

"Hello?"

"Ethan, where are you?" It's Myra.

"Dean and I are at dinner. Why?"

"Is Cale with you?"

"No, I haven't seen him at all today."

"Did he come home last night?" There's worry in her voice.

"I don't think so. I got in really late. He wasn't with you? What's going on?"

"I haven't seen him either. He hasn't answered my calls or texts, and he's not at your apartment. I think something's wrong."

Behind the Book: Fuse: Omertà

Thanks for reading! I hope you enjoyed the second book in the Fuse series! The second book in a new series is always hard. When I sat down to write *The Harvest Moon*, the second book in the Under the Moon series, I was a little worried about writing something that compared to *The Full Moon*. That wasn't the case with *Omertà*. I was actually really excited to dig into the series further and uncover even more of the city of Olympia and also build on Ethan's mission as Fuse. Plus, I had left some cliffhangers in *Origin* that I needed to resolve in this book.

I feel like I've really hit a stride with this series. I know the characters inside and out. I know the story. I know the city. And I'm looking forward to where it's headed in the future.

Actually, this book came together very fast. I wrote the first draft in June 2017 and sent it off to my editor by October after a couple rounds of edits myself. Previously, it would take me six months to a year to write a book from start to finish!

Some people (my mother, for instance) worry that the faster I write these books, the crappier they'll be (to be blunt). I don't think that's the case. In fact, I think they're better. I'm completely immersing myself in the world of Fuse. The day after I finished final edits for *Origin*, I moved right into working on *Omertà*, and now I'll move right into *Oblivion*. It's better than having to reread and reacquaint myself with where the characters are and where the story left off.

Origin is obviously Fuse's origin story. It showed how he got his powers and set up his mission for the whole series. Of course there's a story arc that's cleared up in that book, but really it's setting the stage for a story arc that takes place over the course of the first three books in the series.

In *Omertà*, the stage was already set. It literally picks up in the middle of a scene that ended the first book. With it, I got to explore Ethan grieving Emma, moving on from her sooner than he thought he would, feeling guilty about it, accepting it, and finally coming to terms with his feelings and his sexuality. Very heavy things and that last one especially scared me.

Did I do it right? Will superhero fiction readers take to an LGBT storyline like comic book readers have? Am I telling too much of an emotional story and less of an action story? Will this storyline put off readers I meet in person? Should I label it as an LGBT book? Is it even an LGBT book? Will that hurt the sales for the book?

Ultimately, I think it's an interesting twist on the typical "damsel in distress" trope that's seen in basically every superhero story. Dean is certainly not someone who needs to be saved day after day. He helped save Ethan in *Origin* and Ethan helped save him in *Omertà*. Plus, I had written so many strong female characters in the Under the Moon series and my romance books that I wanted to take a break from it.

I'm still a little scared of the angle I took in this book, but these types of feelings happen in real life. Especially in today's world. Besides, doing something that scares you a little bit is how you grow, right?

I'm very proud of this book and the way this series is shaping up. As of this writing, the first draft of *Oblivion* is done, but it needs work. *A lot* of work. Once it's done, though, it'll fit right

Behind the Book

in with the other two Fuse books. I can't wait for you guys to read it!

Before I officially close out this book, I'd like to thank you for reading. *Origin* was really the first book that I saw consistent daily sales and I really felt like I had done something right. I'm sure *Omertà* will follow suit. It's always great to know that something you put so much time and energy into is paying off and people are enjoying the stories you're writing. So if you keep reading, I'll keep writing.

Finally, if you enjoyed this book (or any of my books), please leave a review online. I read all of them and I love seeing how much you're enjoying my books. Or, if you didn't, what wasn't working for you. I won't know unless you leave a review.

Thanks again for reading! If you haven't already, please join my mailing list to be notified when my next book is out!

DavidNethBooks.com/Newsletter

———

Ethan still doesn't know what happened to his missing brother four months ago. No idea where he went, who took him, or where to find the answers. But then he discovers Fizz, a mutant who's acid spit can melt off a man's face, and he has a new lead.

Meanwhile, Carlo Martelli is in a rage. His cousin's murder can only be a threat to his rule in the local mafia. The immediate suspect is the traitorous Michael Bello who ratted him out to the police. As the mob war erupts, Fuse finds himself in the cross-hairs, which may have been a trap for him all along.

———

Available in ebook, paperback, and audio!
DavidNethBooks.com/Oblivion

More by the Author

To find the rest of the author's books visit
DavidNethBooks.com/Books

———

Subscribe to his newsletter to be the first to know of new
releases and special deals!
DavidNethBooks.com/Newsletter

———

If you enjoyed the book, please consider leaving a review on
Goodreads or the retailer you bought it from. Reviews help
potential readers determine whether they'll enjoy a book, so
any comments on what you thought of the story would be very
helpful!

About the Author

David Neth is the author of the Fuse series, the Small Town Christmas series, the Under the Moon series, and other stories. He lives in Batavia, NY, where he dreams of a successful publishing career and opening his own bookstore.

———

Follow the author at

www.DavidNethBooks.com
www.facebook.com/DavidNethBooks
www.twitter.com/DavidNethBooks
www.instagram.com/dneth13

www.ingramcontent.com/pod-product-compliance
Lightning Source LLC
Chambersburg PA
CBHW032009180726
48283CB00008B/2601